# SUMMER BOY

## TL TRAVIS

SAPPHIRE PUBLISHING

Published by Sapphire Publishing

Formatting by TL Travis

Cover by Cate Ashwood

Photographer: Eric McKinney / 6:12 Photography

https://www.612photog.com

Instagram: Mannequin612

Cover Model: Owen L

Second Issue 2023

# SUMMER BOY

# CONTENTS

Also By

# CHAPTER ONE

**Jonah**

H ello, my name is Jonah Thomas.

Loner.

Loser.

Nineteen going on twenty and still living at home.

I have no fucking clue what I want to do with my life.

Have you ever heard anything more pitiful than that?

Every summer, for as long as I could remember, played on repeat. An endless loop of...nothingness. It'd been this way since I was old enough to operate a cash register. Working at Ahoy Matey's Burgers and Fries, a restaurant that my folks owned on the waterfront at Booth Bay Harbor in Stoney Brook, Maine, was not my life's dream. And before you ask, yes, that *really* is what they named the place. You'd think they would have come up with something more, I don't know—catchy? Mature? Not so easily mocked? Their love of water and boats sure shone through in it though. It was what it was, and this was my life.

The Tall Ship Festival was coming up, during which we'd be slammed. It was the same thing every year, the town packed to near explosion with vacationers out looking to spot the infamous Jack Sparrow. Newsflash, people, he isn't here. He's in Hollywood soaking it up in his McMansion, enjoying the warm sun, bright skies, and caviar served to him on a silver platter. What did I get? Kids running around screaming, poking each other with their plastic pirate swords. Same shit, different year, and I was more than over it.

"Stop leaning on the counter looking bored, Jonah. It's bad for business," my father scolded from behind me for the umpteenth time, sounding like a broken record. "Go wipe down the tables out front."

With a heavy sigh, I grabbed the bucket of solution and a fresh rag, then headed out the side door of the narrow building and toward the outside dining area. The screen door rattled shut behind me. There were no indoor seats, not enough space, only the picnic tables and benches out front, which was why we were only open during the summer months. We stayed open long enough to work through whatever inventory was left or when we got down to just a few things we had space for at home. After that, we closed until it warmed up the following May. No one in their right mind would want to eat an icicle burger while freezing their nuts off in December. Winters here were long, cold, and beyond boring. Stuck inside for the most part was how those of us who didn't ski or snowboard spent them. I longed for the days of summer but wished they didn't include a barrage of hyperactive sightseers.

After high school graduation, just over a year ago, most of the kids I attended with immediately left for college. They couldn't get out of this dinky place fast enough. Me? Well, I had no clue what I wanted to do with my life, and still don't. About the only thing I had a drive for was playing video games, and since math wasn't my forte, I wouldn't be diving into video game design in this lifetime. Besides, my parents didn't have the money for college and my grades were mediocre at best, nixing any chance for a scholarship. So here I was, living the deep-fried dream no one wanted for themselves, soaking up rays as I cleaned up after patrons and dodged seagull shit.

*Living the dream.*

*If only I had one.*

"Jonah," my mother called out, "can you come help your dad unload the delivery truck?"

"Yeah, Mom, be right there." I hoofed it back inside and put away the cleaning supplies. She stayed up front, waiting on the handful of customers we had, while Dad and I filled up the walk-in fridge and freezer. We expected to be swamped this weekend, so Dad had ordered enough to feed the entire town five times over.

"Just think, Jonah, one day all this will be yours when your mother and I retire and move to Florida."

I grimaced. This place was their dream, not mine, but I didn't dare say that. Hurting either one of my parents was something I'd never do, at least not on purpose. I was a late-in-life *surprise* pregnancy. My parents didn't think they could have kids after years of unsuccessfully trying. My mom was floored when she went in for her annual woman's visit and instead of her doctor wishing her a "happy fortieth birthday, see you again next year," she got a "happy birthday, see you in eight weeks for your first ultrasound" in place of it. Shocked and dazed, she left the car idling when she pulled up in front of the house and hopped out to run inside and tell my dad the good news. The vehicle started to roll backward, and she screamed as she jumped back in through the open door she'd thankfully forgotten to shut and slid it into Park, tapping the emergency brake for good measure before resuming her sprint into the house.

Yeah, I've heard this story a time...or a thousand. It's hard to get irritated with them for repeating it when they've always been so proud of me. Caring parents I had an unlimited amount of, though they were a bit smothering sometimes. But they loved me unconditionally.

After the lunch crowd died down, Mom and I kept busy refilling the expo station and condiment areas. Dad worked the back kitchen, cleaning the grill and restocking that zone. When the kids that worked the evening shift clocked in, it was time for the three of us to go home. Listen to me, using the word *kids*. I shook my head at myself, sounding like someone twice my age. But as soon as they'd all arrived, Mom, Dad, and I loaded up in the family van and headed up the hill toward home. Was that any better? Not to my ears, I still sounded like an old man. Who says up the hill anymore, even when it's in the literal sense? Ugh, I really needed to get out and meet people my own age.

Holly was still in high school, so the part-time hours worked well for her. She operated the register, taking orders and handling the customers. Stuart was our night shift manager. He was currently doing online college courses while working toward a business degree. Sometimes I envied him even though a business degree wasn't for me, but a dream was a dream and mine was still a...*blank*.

It was a never-ending battle where Holly was concerned, as I maneuvered around her continual flirting. She was cute and all, but I dunno, I just wasn't interested. I concluded a long time ago, when the crowd I hung out with in high school started pairing off and discussing what base they'd achieved with their latest conquests, that something was wrong with me. None of the girls that went to my school, or guys for that matter, did it for me. No arousal. No need to kiss and see if I felt anything. It was like I was numb, sexually. At that point, I had no shared interest in what they did, and my lack of participation in their "guess who I did last night" conversations resulted in me no longer being invited to hang out with them.

*I was truly broken.*

"Jonah?" My mother asked once we'd parked. "You were awfully quiet on the drive home."

"That took all of five minutes, Mom," I replied, rolling my eyes even though she couldn't see them.

"What do kids your age do for fun?" she continued. Either she hadn't heard my reply, or she chose to ignore it.

"No clue."

My father decided to jump in, pointing out the obvious flaws with his offspring. "You've never had many friends, Jonah." Could've done without his commentary. "You should look into online business classes with the local community college. Ask Stuart, he can probably help you get signed up."

"Huh?"

"Jonah," my father sighed. "Sometimes I swear my voice goes in one ear and right out the other without you absorbing a single word I've said. You'll need to take over the restaurant when your mother and I retire and move to Florida. Possessing a strong business acumen will make things easier for you."

"Florida?"

"Florida," he replied. "We aren't spring chickens anymore, son. And we don't plan to work until we're old and wrinkled. The long, cold winters wreak havoc on your mother's arthritis, and I am too damn old to keep shoveling snow." I bit my tongue, deciding that it was best to not correct him. He hadn't shoveled snow since I was twelve, when he'd handed me the shovel and said, "Yours now, I'm going back for more coffee."

The garage door closed behind us and we all walked through the door that led to the kitchen. "Dad," I began, rethinking the thoughts I had nearly blurted out before. This had to be worded just right or it wasn't gonna fly. "I appreciate your trust in me, I really do. But running the restaurant isn't where I see my future." Both he and Mom turned and stared at me like I'd sprouted a second head before they proceeded to take a seat. I sat down in my usual spot at the dinner table, between them. "Have you considered selling it? You've mentioned Florida a few times now, and honestly, unless you don't want me to go with you, I'd rather be there too. I've had enough of the cold. Plus..."

"Plus what, Jonah?" Mom asked.

"Plus, I've never felt Stoney Brook was the place for me." The deafening silence that met my admission was unnerving.

"I don't know what to say, Jonah," Dad replied. "I guess we figured you'd want to stay here."

"Stay here with what?" I questioned, gesturing wildly around with my hand. "With you guys gone, I'll have no one here but my girl, Sadie." Right on cue, she barked. The love of my life, my three-year-old chocolate lab my parents got me for my sixteenth birthday. Thinking back, I wondered if they felt bad for their lonely son and bought me a friend. I'll never have a more loyal one than Ms. Sadie, that's for sure, so I had nothing to complain about.

"I'm gonna take Sadie for a walk. Come on, girl." My parents said nothing, just sat there, staring at each other across the table. They did that quite often, carrying on conversations wordlessly. Guess when you've been with someone long enough, you eventually get into their head-space and can predict their thoughts.

Sadie and I headed toward the docks, to an area where rogue driftwood waded in, coming in with the high tide, then stayed behind. She sniffed at the bushes as we walked, familiar with the path we often tread. *Alone*. Well, just the two of us. I picked up a stick along the way, I loved to toss them out into the ocean for Sadie to retrieve. Crazy pup, she was a water dog through and through. I whistled and she hopped up from the space where she was digging nearby in the sand, her brown nose covered in it. Probably looking for a crab to torment. Tail wagging, she came to me and sat at my feet as I'd taught her. "Wanna fetch?" I asked her, holding the stick up. "Well, do ya?" She barked once, another trick that took no time for her to learn. I tossed it into the water, then took a seat on the largest log and watched as she swam off after it.

Living this close to the water was great, but there were only a handful of weeks during the year we could enjoy it. Sure, it was always here, but the below-freezing temperatures kept me away in the winter, and I missed it. Florida would offer year-round water experiences, a huge draw for me. What gave my parents the idea I wanted to stay behind was beyond me. I guessed, if they were ready for me to move out, I could get a job and my own place down there. I'd saved nearly every penny they paid me, only spending small amounts here and there on video games and whatnot. With my experience, it'd probably be easy to get a job working in a restaurant anywhere we ended up. I could cook, run the register, stock, manage inventory—you name it, I did it. Pretty much everything but payroll and paying bills.

I decided that's how I needed to approach this with them—point out the positives.

With that thought in mind, I whistled for Sadie to return. Needed to strike while my thoughts were hot. She hit the sand running and stopped right in front of me, where she broke out into a full-body shake. Now both of us were soaked. "Gee, thanks, girl." She barked, and I patted her head. "Time to go home."

"Mom, Dad?" I called out as Sadie and I came inside.

"Out back, son."

I headed their way, taking the porch steps two at a time. They were chilling in the Adirondack chairs. Our backyard had a fantastic view of the water. Huh, seemed I was a water dog, too, since that's immediately where my mind went.

"What're you grinning about?"

"So, I had a thought," I began. They rolled their eyes. Now I knew just how ridiculous it looked when I did it. "Just hear me out, please?"

Dad swept his hand through the air. "The floor is yours."

"I'm sure you are ready for me to move out, and I get that. But leaving me behind would suck. What if I promise to get a job right away and then I can get my own place?" I stated, pleading my case. Ever the loser, begging my parents to take me with them when I should be dancing for joy at the prospect of being on my own. So not a normal nineteen-year-old.

Mom smiled at me. "Jonah, you moving out or us becoming empty nesters was never given a single thought. We figured that, with us gone, maybe you'd want to venture out, spread your wings, have some fun. It has never been about not wanting you to live with us. I guess this is on your father and me, we should have talked to you about this first and not made decisions for you. And for that, we're sorry. If you want to move with us, then that's what we'll do. Honestly, I like having you near."

Dad nodded his agreement. "Son, trust me. We'd be worried sick every second of the day if we moved without you, wondering if you're eating and taking care of yourself. Yes, we know you're a man now and can do all these things, but being a parent doesn't mean you stop caring or worrying when your kids become adults. You've always been my best friend and I agree wholeheartedly with your mother, we'd love to have you with us in Florida."

"Yeah?" I questioned, making sure this wasn't them doing the whole parental guilt thing.

"Son, nothing would make us happier."

# CHAPTER TWO

**Micah**

"Remind me again how I let you talk me into going on this family road trip when I could be sitting on the beach right now?" I complained, easily for the fiftieth time since we left this morning. "Wouldn't it have been quicker and less painful to fly?"

It didn't work. I was still trapped in the car with my parents, sitting in the back seat next to my twelve-year-old sister. I could've been living it up with my friends in Daytona this weekend. Surf, sand, hotties in swimsuits, countless willing bodies to please and be pleased by. Flesh as far as the eye could see. That was how I would've preferred to spend my last summer before entering my final year of college and then being thrust into the cruel world of adulthood.

My mom sighed. "Micah, enough. This is likely our last family vacation. Can you at least humor me and pretend to enjoy our company? Yes, flying was quicker, but I wanted a road trip with you kids."

*Le sigh.*

She was right, but I couldn't find it in me to care because the maximum suckage that went along with this whole lame-ass vacation idea consumed me. I was like an angry green monster, trying to break out, go on a rampage. My sister Addison shifted beside me, purposely blowing bubbles with her chewing gum and smacking her lips like a fucking Neanderthal. "Addy, seriously. Do you need to sound like such a pig?" She stared me down, blew another big bubble, and *smack*.

*Ugh.*

"Who decided a trip to Maine in an SUV with a family of four was the right one for us?" It's like I couldn't control myself. Suddenly I was back to being twelve, as well, and lacked the ability to filter my thoughts or bite my tongue.

*Two weeks.* Two fucking weeks of this to endure. Even sharing a hotel room with my sister, for God's sake. I mean, seriously. How many circles would this be for Dante? Oh, wait, it would be all nine!

Two days in the car.

With my family.

To Maine, then back to Florida.

Twenty-two hours.

Forty-four hours round trip.

Shoot. Me. Now.

"Micah, you know it was your sister's turn to pick our summer vacation destination. You had your turn last year," my dad reminded me, his eyes never leaving the road. He was cautious on the best of days and even more so when the entire family accompanied him.

As If I would have forgotten.

"Yes, and we went to freaking Cabo. That was the bomb!" I turned to Addy. "You know Johnny Depp won't be there, right?" I asked, more to be a dickhead than anything else. My mental stability continued to haul ass in reverse to the point my parents now had two twelve-year-olds along for the ride. Lucky them! "He has better things to do than play pretend with you."

She stuck her tongue out at me. "I know that. I'm not stupid. I just thought the boats looked cool."

"Where are we anyway?" I asked, nearly channeling my inner Bart Simpson—*Are we there yet? Are we there yet?*—until we magically pulled up to our destination or my parents dropped me off at the nearest bus station. The latter would probably be more likely to happen, and I'm not sure the bus is for me. Might be in my best interest to take it down a notch or two.

"Just outside of Washington D.C. We're staying the night in Baltimore, so we have about an hour more," Dad replied. I figured Mom had had enough of me when she scowled at her phone screen, madly attacking the keys as she turned away to face forward. I'm sure bitching to her friend Beverly about the vast level of immaturity I'd reached. Whatever.

I know, I know, enjoy the time you have with your family because one day, they'll be gone. But when you're young it's hard to remember that. I attended Florida State University in Tallahassee and lived in the dorms on campus, but I did try to come home during most breaks unless my friends and I had shit planned. I stared out into the dark night, thinking about the last three years. I'd be graduating with a bachelor's degree in finance next May. Numbers were my thing, always had been. I toyed around with the idea of going back for my MBA, but I really needed a break from school for a bit first. Understanding mathematics and equations came easily to me, but knowing I was about to enter a world of permanent number crunching wasn't as inviting as it once was, though I'd never tell my parents that. They had already spent a metric fuckton on my tuition and housing.

My father was a personal injury lawyer and had hoped I'd follow in his footsteps, join his firm. Was he disappointed in me for not doing so? Not at all. A little bummed out, yes, but he got it, the lawyer thing wasn't for me. My mom was a math teacher at Addy's grade school, the same one I had attended. She was probably the parent I got my love of numbers from. I hated having to call her Mrs. Hannigan back then, it sounded ridiculous when I did. Unfortunately, that was the rule, no matter how much I bitched about it. Hmm, bitching seems to be a theme for me. I'll just keep that little revelation locked away.

Outside of my smart mouth, I'd never rocked the boat or caused any real trouble, so they never enforced rules or punishments on me. I was the first to admit I'd had it pretty easy, though I had a feeling the same wasn't going to be said for Addy. She was already pushing their buttons and she'd not even hit her teen years. Yeah, Addy and I argued—our differing personalities and the age difference guaranteed that—but I'd always be there for her no matter what. Although her obnoxious gum-chewing habit was testing that love.

Before I had the chance to dive any further down memory lane, we pulled up in front of the hotel. "We're here," my mother sang, "and Mama needs an extra-large glass of wine." I breathed a sigh of relief as I got out and stretched my legs, feeling the need for a shot of something strong myself.

"Alright, everyone, grab your suitcases. Let's go," Dad directed.

Who knew traveling would wear you out this much? As soon as my ass hit the bed, I turned to mush. Addy mumbled something about showering first, but I was too tired to give a shit. She came out of the bathroom, who knows how much later, only to find me in the same position I'd landed in.

"The restroom is yours, your highness." She bowed like the smartass she was. I rolled my eyes, grabbed my toiletry bag and a pair of basketball shorts, and took my turn in the shower.

"Jesus," I muttered aloud, using my foot to scoot the various towels Addy had left across the floor. "She's worse than a frat house." I grabbed a clean one from the stack, not trusting what Addy did with the wadded-up ones, and wiped the steam from the mirror.

"Damn, I look haggard as fuck." When my parents woke us up at six a.m. and said we had fifteen minutes to get in the car, there'd been no time to primp. On a normal day, I'm a good-looking guy, if I do say so myself. I can walk into a bar and walk out with the guy of my choice ten minutes later. But today, looking as I did, it was highly unlikely anyone would give the bags under my eyes a second look, let alone tell me their name. And what the fuck was I even wearing?

I scowled and glanced down at the old-as-fuck grey sweats and holey-ass threadbare anime tee I had on. Yeah, not a good look. Seems dressing in the dark was not something I excelled at. Good thing my folks opted to eat in the car and keep to the schedule as opposed to dining inside a restaurant along the way. They might've tagged me as a street urchin and labeled my parents model citizens for feeding those in need.

When was the last time I even got laid?

Random thought but, given my current attire, one that warranted answering. Who knows, but I sure as hell wasn't gonna jerk it while sharing a room with my sister. Maybe I could find someone to blow off a little road-trip steam with when we got to Maine. A lonely lumberjack? The quiet teacher, silently reading in the café? Hmm...

I came out of the bathroom and entered a dark room, the illumination from my sister's iPad the only light. After I got situated, I did the same with my phone. Scrolling through social media, I jealously went quickly past the photos my friends posted of the trip I was supposed to be on. *Lucky bastards*. Depressed the hell out of me.

Ugh. I tossed my phone on the nightstand separating our beds and crashed. All too soon, my dad was pounding on the door separating our two rooms while my mother repeatedly called our cell phones, one after the other, until either Addy or myself answered.

I unlocked the door from our side and threw it open. "We're up, and now I'm sure the rest of the damn floor is, too."

"Watch your mouth, son," my father scolded, but I was too tired, uncaffeinated, and angry to care.

Addy grabbed her clothes and bolted into the bathroom before I had a chance. Times like this reminded me how lucky we were to have our own bathrooms at home. Thirty painstaking minutes later, we left for the second leg of our fun-filled family journey.

*Not!*

By the time we reached the hotel in Maine, we'd stopped no less than a dozen times for someone who needed to pee or someone else who needed to eat, or for my mother to take pictures. The ten-hour drive had turned into twelve when it finally came to an end.

An overenthusiastic guy whose nametag read "Ben" greeted us. "Welcome to the Stoney Brook Inn. How may I assist you?" There was no way he was that fucking happy to be sitting behind a hotel desk. Guy had to be toking between guest arrivals.

"Yes, hello, Ben," my father replied. "James Hannigan, we have two adjoining suites booked."

"Ah, yes. You're on the third floor for ten nights. I just need your credit card and ID, please. How many keys for each room would you like, sir?"

While Dad finished checking us in, I walked around the lobby, taking it all in. The wall of glass at the front of the building provided a panoramic view of the town. The smattering of lights below made it look...what's the word I was looking for? Quaint? Picturesque? Yeah, my creative writing teacher wasn't fond of me, to say the least, but my math teachers loved me. Just beyond the lights, it was pitch black, and if I had to guess, that was the ocean. I loved the water, practically grew up on it, skiing, boogie boarding, snorkeling. Getting dive-certified was on my bucket list, but it was far too expensive at this point in my life. It was going to happen someday, even if I had to work two jobs to make it a reality.

"We offer coffee and breakfast grab-and-go snacks in the morning, from seven to nine in the lobby," I overheard Ben say. "If you need something more, there are plenty of restaurants within walking distance. Elevator is to your right."

"Thank you," Dad told him. "Kids," he called out, "let's head upstairs."

Unlike last night, I was wide awake and ready to hit the town, even though this one looked a little sleepy from the hill we were currently perched on. When we got to our rooms, set up with a connecting door like our hotel on the road the night before, we unpacked and got comfortable since we'd be in town for an extended period of time. Addy grabbed the remote and started flipping through channels while I googled our home away from home to see if it had anything exciting to offer, nightlife or otherwise.

After a few minutes, I resigned myself to the fact that there wasn't much to the town that time forgot, so I tossed my phone aside, opened my iPad, and started reading until I finally drifted off to sleep. I woke the next morning to one of our parents once again pounding away on the shared door, giving us their usual "fifteen minutes to get ready" spiel. That shit was getting old fast.

Once we were all ready, it was off to breakfast with the family at a restaurant down the road and within walking distance, as everything was, according to the attendant at the front desk this morning. "No need to take your car, might as well leave it here and walk." I snickered at his comment, so similar to the little stoner from the evening before. There's no way that little dweeb hadn't been high. And was the walking bit meant to be some sort of selling point?

After we ate, we headed toward the shops that Mom wanted to check out, but when we reached Main Street, we opted to go our separate ways. My sister was anxious to see the big ships and Mom wanted to window-shop along the way to the docks. Personally, I just wanted to look around, see if maybe they had a place somewhere to rent a boogie board so I could catch a wave or two. I mean, this place was cute and all, but there wasn't much life to it from my perspective. At least, not that I had noticed.

# CHAPTER THREE

**Jonah**

As soon as we rolled up the shades at eleven, I saw that the line of customers that had started to form while we prepared to open now ran through the center of the seating area and down and around the pathway. Visitors came from far and wide for this weekend's Tall Ship Festival, and it appeared they all wanted fried food. Main Street was shut off to vehicles, only open to foot traffic. Our restaurant was located directly behind it, so the only traffic in front of us was walkers. Luckily for us, the alleyway separating the row we were on from the main thoroughfare was where our deliveries came in. Today, the local crafters had sat up their merchandise tents along the street, readying for the influx of shoppers for the vendor fair portion of the festival.

My parents had been smart when they opened this business, more than ten years before I was born. They owned the building outright along with our house, which had belonged to my mom's parents before them. In my opinion, and with no family outside of the three of us left, it was time to move on. Not that my take on it mattered, but there it was. They hadn't said anything more about moving to Florida since our last conversation, and it was driving me crazy.

I was ready to *go*.

"Number twenty-seven," I called out from the pickup window. Mom and I had swapped places, so she now took the orders while I worked fulfillment. "Condiments are to your right," I told the girl who picked up the tray of food. I barely made eye contact anymore, able to do this job with little to no thought, having done it for as long as I had. When the line finally died down, Dad made the three of us lunch. He and Mom took theirs to the office while I stayed up front.

I had my back turned and was refilling my cup when someone rang the service bell. "Welcome to Ahoy Matey's, how can I help you?" I rattled off without looking up.

"Wow, if you sounded any more excited, I might just pee my pants," some smartass answered.

I turned quickly, readying myself to unleash and point out that he and his soiled pants could head down the boardwalk to find something else to eat, when I came face to face with the most gorgeous human I'd ever encountered. His eyes, so unique, were unlike any I'd ever seen. I swear, I fucking gasped, ridiculous as that might sound.

"Hello"—he glanced down at my nametag—"Jonah." Glad he did that. Had I needed to recite my own name, I'm not sure I could have. "What do you recommend?" My level of dysfunction increased as I again said nothing, only pointed to the signage overhead. "A man of few words I see. Hmm." He perused the menu while I shamelessly gawked at him. "I'll take the shrimp basket with fries and a large Mr. Pibb."

I nodded and rang up his order, not saying a word. Didn't really need to, since the part of the cash register that faced him lit up with his total. "Thank you, Jonah," he said when I handed him his change and order number.

Immediately, I ran to the back to make his food. Never had I been so tongue-tied by another living, breathing soul, nor had I ever before experienced a million fricking butterflies running rampant through my guts. Vomiting was inevitable.

*Get it together, Jonah. He's just a guy.*

*Yeah, a totally freaking drop-dead gorgeous one.*

*Deep breath, you've got this.*

Was I freaking out because he was a male or because another human had finally piqued my interest? Both, possibly. I wasn't sure if the way I felt now was better than the ache of being broken, numb. Either way, I was a mess.

With trembling hands, I assembled his basket, my nerves out of freaking control. How I didn't spill his food, I'll never know. I walked over to the pickup window and called out his number.

"So, Jonah, what time do you get off?"

"Huh?" *Brilliant response, Jonah. Stupid. Stupid. Stupid.*

"Work. What time is your shift over?" he clarified. "By the way, I'm Micah."

*Micah,* I inwardly sighed. At least, I hoped it wasn't outward.

"Uh, five?"

"Was that a question?" Micah smiled, flashing a perfect set of pearly whites. This guy had to have flaws, right?

I shook my head to clear the waves of stupidity that fogged it. "Sor—sorry. I, um, I get off at five." I wiped my sweaty palms on my apron.

"And what does one do for fun in the town of Stoney Brook?"

"Fun?" I repeated, my inner parrot once again showing its face.

He laughed, "Yes, Jonah. Fun. You do have it, don't you? If I had to guess, I'd say we're around the same age?"

"I'm nineteen, twenty in October," I blurted out. Like he really cared when my birthday was. It took everything in me not to slide to the floor and disappear from view.

"I'm twenty." He smiled. "I'll be twenty-one in September."

"Jonah." I jumped at my mother's voice, unaware she was nearby. A knowing smirk adorned her face. "Why don't you take a break? Go chat with your new friend."

*New friend.*

Embarrassed wasn't a strong enough word to cover how horrified I was by her comment, though I knew she didn't mean anything negative by it. My parents were old school and that's how things were back in their days. Was I looking for a new friend, or hoping for something more? *Hopefully, he doesn't see how desperately lonely I am...*

"Is that okay?" I asked Micah. This guy's smile could melt wax, I swear.

"I think that's a great idea," Micah replied. "Meet you over there." He pointed to the farthest table out.

"Breathe, Jonah." Mom smiled and patted my shoulder after he'd walked away. "He's just a boy."

My parents and I had never once had a gender preference conversation, or any birds-and-bees one, for that matter. Probably because I'd never shown any interest in anyone before. My mother didn't seem bothered by the prospect of my favoring the male species. Great, now I sounded like the narrator from those wildlife documentaries Dad binge-watched. Now, though, my face was hot, and I was nervous as hell. It was like having flu symptoms. If this was what it felt like to be interested in someone, I wasn't sure I cared to explore it much further. I swallowed my pride and nodded at my mom, grabbed my soda, and headed out front, taking the seat across from him. *Micah*.

"Do you want Old Bay? Malt vinegar? Ketchup?" I stood, ready to grab whatever he wanted.

"I'm good, Jonah. But thanks." He took a sip of his drink, and my eyes were glued to his lips as they wrapped around the straw. I'd never been jealous of a straw before now. Was it possible to feel an emotion toward an inanimate object? 'Cause I sure as hell did. I shivered, like full-body chills, and had to shift because, well...*Ugh*. Bad time for my dick to take notice. "So," Micah began again. "Back to my previous question, what is there to do for fun around here?"

"Honestly, I don't do much outside of work and play with Sadie." Having admitted that aloud definitely labeled me a dork.

"Sadie?" Micah asked. He seemed sad about that. "Is that your girlfriend?"

"Ha. Nah, no girlfriend." Micah sighed. *Hmm, interesting*. "Sadie's my lab. Loves the water, so we hang out down here most nights, play fetch. I throw the stick into the bay, she dives in and brings it back. I know, lame," I muttered, feeling like a fool for the word vomit I'd just spewed all over him.

"Actually, that sounds like fun. We never really had pets growing up. Well, nothing more than my sister's cat and a couple of hamsters. Nothing you can play fetch with or take on walks. At least, I wouldn't want to be the one to try and put a leash on a cat. Never had a dog, though. I always wanted one," Micah replied. "Sadie and I have that in common, I'm a water dog, too. I didn't see any surf or boogie board rental shops nearby, though. Did I miss them?"

"There aren't any," I told him.

"What?! How can you be this close to the water and not be able to rent any toys to enjoy it with?" He shook his head, incredulous.

I shrugged. "No clue. I love the water, too, but I've never been surfing. Or waterskiing, for that matter." Thinking back, no one ever invited me out on their ski boats during summer break. We had a boat that my dad and I used for fishing, but it only had a trolling motor on it, and we never left the bay area.

"Prime aquatic real estate going to waste," Micah complained, shaking his head.

"Well, the most excitement we get around here is when Merle and George, the local drunks, decide to race each other in an inebriated swim-off to see who can reach the middle first," I told him.

He glanced out at the water. "The middle of what? There's nothing but blue as far as the eye can see."

"Exactly."

"Whoa."

"We don't have a lifeguard on duty unless it's a high-traffic weekend like this one, and they're all locals who volunteer for the events anyway. When the usual troublemakers get drunk and pull their stunts, they're so loud, they wake up half the town. Whoever's closest grabs their fishing boats and heads out to retrieve their dumb asses. Guess that's about the only excitement we get around here," I said. I wracked my brain for something else to share—hopefully, something less pathetic than what had just come out of my mouth. There was no way this guy could ever be interested in a small-town boy like me. "Well, I guess I'll get back to work. It was nice meeting you, Micah."

"You said five, right?" he asked.

"Huh?" I seemed to be saying that a lot. Was it even a word or more of an obscure sound? I shrugged off that thought before it became a rabbit hole of epic proportions and turned back to the conversation at hand.

"When you get off. You said five, right?" Micah repeated.

"Um, yeah."

"Sweet. Well, since you said you don't do much for fun, I'm guessing you don't have plans for tonight, then?' He smiled and my stomach flip-flopped. "Meet you here at five?"

*What did I do right?* "I need to go home and let Sadie out."

"Bring her with. Do you live far?" Micah asked, and if I wasn't mistaken, he seemed excited at the prospect of spending time with us.

"Just at the top of the hill," I said, pointing in the general direction. "About a five-minute drive."

"Great," Micah answered as he threw his trash away. "I'll give you time to do the family dinner thing. Meet back here at five-thirty?"

I nodded, unable to find my words. This guy, this total stranger wanted to hang out with me. What was I missing? "Better make it six. I reek of onions and grease so I'm gonna need to shower first."

"Alright, it's a date." Just as Micah said that, a girl nearby called out his name. "Oh, there's my family. I'll see you later."

*Date?*

I managed to reply with a simple, "Yeah." I was incapable of anything more. He waved and headed in the direction of three people staring me down while I stood rooted in place. Fear of moving, of waking up and finding none of this had happened, kept me rooted as I watched Micah and the three others with him disappear into the crowds lining the waterfront.

"Jonah?" Mom called out from the front window.

"Coming."

# Chapter Four

**Micah**

*This is just a summer fling.*

*This is just a summer fling.*

Then why did my heart race and my stomach find a new home in my throat when I saw him and his dog nearing?

"Hey," I said to Jonah as I bent to extend my hand for Sadie to sniff. She spent about a millisecond doing so before she licked it. "She's beautiful," I told him, scratching her head. Her tail wagged faster with each pass of my hand. "You're a happy girl, aren't you," I praised. She barked and gave me a doggy grin. "Oh man, she's so awesome."

"That's my girl." Jonah proudly beamed.

"Well, show me what you two crazy kids do during your fun time."

We set off and walked along the edge of the waterfront, over to the end where trees stood nearby, where we came to a large piece of driftwood and took a seat. Jonah pulled out a stick he must have hidden at some point during a previous visit and tossed it out into the water. Sadie bounded in after it without a care in the world. "Wow, you weren't kidding. She didn't even dip a toe or a paw in first to test the temperature." Jonah laughed, the happy lilt drawing me in. So light, so carefree. So different from the nervous guy I had lunch with. Maybe I just needed to get him away from work to draw out his personality. Mentally rubbing my hands together, I thought, *Challenge accepted*. I was on a mission to draw Jonah out of his shell.

"Yeah, she's kind of great," Jonah admitted.

"So, tell me about yourself."

"Not much to tell. You saw where I work, which is where I spend most of my life. My parents own the restau-

rant so I've worked there for as long as I can remember."
Jonah shrugged and stared down at his feet.

"Okay, so we've established that you don't do anything
for fun. But you at least blow off steam from time to time,
don't ya?" I mean, everyone seeks release, right?

He stared blankly at me. Guess I needed to find another
approach.

"Girlfriend?"

"Nope."

"Boyfriend?"

"Nope."

"Fuck buddy? Friend with benefits? Two friends killing
time?"

"Huh?"

Well, shit. I was barking up the wrong vacation fling tree.

"Jonah, are you gay?" I asked. I hated doing that, but his
responses left me in a state of confusion.

"I don't know what I am," he whispered, refusing to
make eye contact. His cheeks pinked with an adorable
tinge of red.

"Have you ever dated?"

"No." He blushed even more. "Never been interested
in anyone. At least, not before now," he mumbled the last
part as he turned toward the water.

"Before now?" Hold it. He found me interesting? Why did hope spring forth when I realized that?

He shrugged again and said nothing.

"Maybe you're ace or demi?" I offered.

"What're those?" he asked, reluctantly making eye contact.

I pulled out my phone and googled the terminology, then handed it over for him to read. "And maybe, you're just you. Jonah." To some, labels were important. To others, not so much. Me? I didn't care either way, as long as all parties involved were happy.

A few moments later, he handed my phone back and wiped his palms on his jeans. "Are you um, are you interested in me?" he asked, turning my own words back on me.

I grinned. "Yeah, I am." That seemed to brighten his mood. He smiled and matching dimples adorned each cheek. This guy was too cute for words and had zero clue just how high he ranked on the fuckability scale. Hell, I'd bet my first year's salary he was untouched in every sense of the word.

We took turns throwing the stick out for Sadie to retrieve while making idle chitchat. The band on the stage in town in the background wasn't too bad. Maybe Jonah would want to watch them one night? This was probably the least stressful date—first meeting? Hang-out?—I'd ever had, however I ended up categorizing it. Granted, we didn't know much about each other, but the question-and-answer portion of the evening was off and running and I was eager for more.

Jonah stood and snagged a couple of flat rocks off the ground that had washed up onto the shore. "How long are you in town for?" he asked, side-arming one to send it skipping across the water.

"Sweet. You got seven skips on that one," I said, joining him. "Like, nine more days? My sister chose this place thinking she'd run into Johnny Depp or some shit."

Jonah laughed. "Seems to be a general theme with visitors. You'd be surprised how many times I hear that each year."

"You have any brothers or sisters?" I asked, tossing a rock of my own. It only skipped four times before it *thunked* and sank.

"Nope, only child. You only have the one sister?" Jonah asked me, releasing another. "Any more?"

"Dude, that one hit, like, ten skips." I paused and tried another. "No more, just the one, which is more than enough. Her name is Addison, Addy for short." This time it only hit three. I was going in the wrong direction in this game.

"Where are you guys visiting from?"

"Florida. I start my senior year of college when we get back, around mid-August, then I'm launched out into the real world." Saying it aloud really made the reality hit home. Kinda scary, if I was being honest. It had been a dream for so long to finally be on my own, out from under my parents' thumbs, and now it was like...*whoa*. Out on my own, away from everything I've known. Paying rent and utilities. Right now, I paid for nothing. What my scholarships didn't cover, my parents did. I'd never had a real job before. How in the hell was I gonna pull off this adulting gig?

*Is it getting hot out here or is it just me?* I tugged at the collar on my shirt, attempting to fan myself with it.

"You okay over there?"

"Oh, um, yeah. Reality just kinda bitch-slapped me. So, tell me, what does the future for Jonah look like?" I needed to get the spotlight off me before anxiety reared its ugly head.

"It's a huge, beyond-gigantic, empty canvas of nothingness." He dropped the rocks in his hand and trudged back over to the log. "I honestly have zero ideas what to do, every day is the same for me. It's like my mind is blocked and can't look past today. What are you majoring in?"

"Finance, the exciting world of numbers. Figured I'd likely have no money of my own for a while, so playing with someone else's could be fun." I waggled my brows, making him laugh.

"Ha-ha. My excitement is not that much better unless you count it as exciting to play video games with the only other eligible person around—my dad. He's tried to play with me, but he doesn't get it and dies within the first five minutes. Every time. But at least he tries, right? I've never seen myself living the college life. School isn't my thing. If I'm gonna be forced to do something, I want to get paid for it. Paying to go to school and being told what to do has literally no appeal for me," he admitted. The sincerity in his voice led me to believe what he said.

"Not everyone finds their path at our ages and not everyone is built for school. Some are well into their thirties before they find what interests them. You can't compare yourself to others. You have to do right by *you*. It's not like you're not doing something, you're working, so there's that," I told him, trying to lessen the blow he had dealt himself.

"True," he replied, staring down at his feet and drawing lines in the sand with the toe of one worn sneaker.

"Hey, look down there." I pointed across the beach. "I see some bonfires. Do you ever come down here at night and just hang out?"

"Nah, never been invited." When he didn't elaborate, I knew there was probably much more to that story. What was wrong with these people? The Jonah I was getting to know was great, so why wouldn't they want to hang out with him?

"This is a public beach, so no invitation is required." I stood and took his hand, practically dragging him toward the bonfires. "Come on, Sadie. Let's go, girl." Even as I called to Jonah's dog, I kept our hands entwined, and he didn't fight to pull away. We walked up to the first bonfire, just kind of checking things out. Nobody said anything about us holding hands or looked uncomfortable with it. Even if they had, it would have meant nothing to me, but I wouldn't want to put Jonah in a situation where he felt uncomfortable. Eventually, someone Jonah knew spotted him and called him over.

"Hey, Jonah!" The guy smiled. "We never see you down here."

I nudged his shoulder and whispered, "See? You just thought other people didn't care. Maybe they actually *do*, and you just gave up on them a bit too soon." Jonah shrugged and waved to the guy as we passed.

We walked along the beachfront from bonfire to bonfire. Visitors and locals alike were having a good time mingling and making new friends. You could tell which were which because residents asked others where they were visiting from, how long were they in town for, what brought them here. Meanwhile, Jonah and I continued on while Sadie followed behind, happily barking out her greetings to everyone. Passersby stopped to pet her and she basked in every minute of it. It was comfortable and quite domestic, like this stroll along the beach with our dog was the norm.

Thoughts of domestication? Not normally my jam.

Who was I, and what happened to Micah Hannigan?

I didn't know what it was about Jonah, but he was nothing like I expected. I had started this believing it was just another hookup for me—a one-and-done like I was used to. Yet this abrupt shift in me, oddly enough, I didn't mind. Change of plans due to a change in *feelings*. Feelings weren't something I did outside of family, yet here I was, going into this as something to pass the time with and now feeling that there was more to build upon. It was kind of nice to have somebody to hang out with and I couldn't lie to myself, I was interested in him. Everything about him pulled me in. When we talked, it was hard to get him to open up and made me wonder if he ever really had anyone to confide in, but little by little, he shared more. I bet there was an extrovert inside screaming to get out.

At this point, we'd reached the end of the sandy part of the beach and moved onto large rock formations I wasn't keen to climb in the dark of night. Not to mention, Sadie wouldn't have been able to follow. The light from the fires behind us illuminated the end of the beachfront. To the left of us, was endless black, stretched out across the Atlantic. In front of us were the mounds of rock and to the right, the asphalt road that would lead us back into the heart of town. For the return trip, we tread the pavement and peeked into the closed shop fronts. The only one that remained open was The Ship's Hull Coffee House. Even the ice cream parlor had closed for the night.

"Which hotel are you staying at?" he asked as we neared the center of town. I pointed to the one at the top of the hill right as you came into town. "Come on, Sadie and I will walk you up."

It didn't take long. Everything was within arm's reach here, and ten minutes later, we found ourselves standing outside of the hotel entrance. Not ready to say goodnight, I grasped for things to talk about, any way to prolong the inevitable. "Do you work tomorrow?" I finally asked Jonah.

"Yeah, I pretty much do every day in the summer. Sometimes, on the weekends, my parents will schedule us off, but with this weekend being what it is, the entire staff will be there. We usually stay busy from open to close during the Tall Ships Festival."

"Oh, bummer. I was hoping we could hang out again," I admitted, surprised by the disappointment I felt at potentially not seeing Jonah.

He grinned and the dimples reappeared. "Whenever you get a break from searching for buried treasure, stop by. If it's not too busy, I can ask my parents if I can take off."

Suddenly, in a surprising role switch, I was the one overcome with a sense of shyness, not Jonah. This wasn't an emotion I knew very well, and I forced myself to shake it off. If I didn't ask for what I wanted, I'd never know, and life was too short to fill it with regrets.

"Jonah, would it be alright if I kissed you?" Nerves and vulnerability shone through my words.

His eyes widened and I wondered if I'd made a terrible mistake, misunderstood what I thought I'd felt brewing between us. As the seconds ticked on, I wished I could retract the words. It was obvious Jonah led a relatively sheltered life and I was moving too fast for him. Just as I'd resigned myself to calling it a night, to tucking tail and heading inside, he surprised me by pressing his lips to mine. My shock quickly settled, replaced by an overwhelming need for more.

I wrapped my arms around his waist and tugged him against me, deepening the kiss. Jonah froze but didn't pull away, so I kept a firm hold and slid my tongue along the crease between his lips. His mouth slightly parted, a move I took as an invitation, and I tentatively entered. *Tread lightly*, was burning through my mind, plus the thought of having my tongue bitten off wasn't appealing. It took him a second to catch on before he followed my lead and his tongue trailed mine. *Was I his first kiss?* That sudden awareness had me second-guessing my sense of worth. *Did I just take what wasn't meant for me?* No, had it not been okay, Jonah wouldn't have initiated the kiss.

*Would he?*

How could I suddenly feel like I wanted so much more from someone I hardly knew? Generally, at this point of the date—or hookup, as it usually was—the kissing would merely be a prelude to fucking. A way for my temporary partner and I to blow off steam between exams or take a much-needed break from mounds of homework and hours of studying. I was struck stupid when I realized that wasn't what I wished to pursue with Jonah. I wanted to take things slow and get to know him, though time wasn't on our side. But the depth of this kiss had so much hidden inside its meaning, like he was giving a part of himself to me, and I actually received it, didn't blow it off. He wasn't a means to an end, this was a door that had sprung open and presented me with something more. Though what that something more was, I wasn't sure I'd ever find out, given the fact I was only in town for nine more days.

Fuck. My. Life.

# Chapter Five

**Jonah**

*H*  *oly shit! My dick is hard!*

Crap, was I supposed to be embarrassed about that? I was too excited over the fact that it was. Micah was hard, too, so I supposed that's a good thing? Should I be freaked out? To many, this wouldn't be a big deal but to me, it was life-changing. Touching dicks through clothes with another guy, though? If it felt right, it must be right because no negative alarms were going off in my brain—just awareness. When we pulled apart, I hurriedly tugged my shirt down to try and hide my erection, just in case Micah had any issues with it.

"Don't do that," Micah said, gently moving my hand away. "It's nothing to be embarrassed about. It's not like you popped wood standing up in front of a classroom filled with your peers."

My eyes widened in horror. "Oh, God, has that happened to you?"

Micah laughed. "No. Thank fuck. Though it may if one of my professors asks me to stand up and share what I did this summer with everyone." He closed in, coming near, and my heart rate escalated.

"What did you do?" I asked, breathlessly. Half of me wanted to know and the other half dreaded what he was about to say. Was I just a means to pass the time for Micah? Could I become the type of guy who engaged in casual sex? Would we even *have* sex? Likely not, considering how long it had taken before another human interested me at all. My mind was swirling with questions and what-if scenarios I'd never dared allowed it to venture into before. Especially not with someone who wasn't a faceless dream, but a living, breathing flesh-and-blood human.

"Well," he began, the palm of his hand resting against the wall just beside my head. A shiver ran through me as my thoughts heated, turned to ones where I was pinned beneath Micah. My gaze locked on his. *Gray. Yes, they're gray.* I'd never met someone with gray eyes before. "Jonah," he whispered, his sultry voice drawing me back. "You're the story, the memory I hope to have from my summer vacation."

"Me?" I squeaked. I cleared my throat and tried again, in a ridiculously deep voice that wasn't mine. "Me?"

God, his smile was something else. "Yes, Jonah. You."

What did he want with me? I couldn't understand what he saw. The two of us had walked past plenty of good-looking men and women along the waterfront. His gaze hadn't lingered on a single one, nor had he flirted with anybody else. Micah held *my* hand, not caring who saw. "Why me?"

"Well, that's a bit open-ended." Micah winked. "For one, you're absolutely adorable. There's something about you that's latched onto me, drawing me in. You're rare. Like a breath of fresh air. I'll admit, I wasn't looking for anything more than a hookup, but as I get to know you better, I want us to spend more time together. Does that make any sense?"

"Yeah." I shrugged, my insecurity screaming that I didn't deserve his attention. "I guess it does. I'm pretty boring, though, outside of Sadie." I glanced down at her on the sidewalk beside us. Her tongue hung to one side as she stared up expectantly, as if to ask why we weren't playing with her. The love I felt for her, my best friend—hell, my only friend—had me smiling. She had a way of making things better. "I play video games and walk my dog. Oh yeah—and work. The three things my life consists of, and even to my own ears, that's boring. There's literally nothing special about me."

He ground his groin against mine. Neither of us was completely erect, but we were still close enough that it wouldn't take much to get either of us there. "I would have to say that our dicks state otherwise."

I swallowed hard, past the lump in my throat. "Yeah, well, this is *all* new to me, so I guess I don't really know what any of it means. But you're only here for a few days, which is kind of a bummer. Like starting something that could never be finished. I'm not gonna lie and say otherwise 'cause it's true." I was proud of myself, speaking my concerns. Normally, I'd clam up and go with the flow. *Normally?* None of this was normal for me, but it was rare I ever went against what someone else wanted. Guess in that sense, I was more of a follower than the leader I probably should be.

"Are you interested in spending more time with me while I'm here, even though it's only for a few more days?" Micah asked. I wish I had a tenth of his courage, even if right now he seemed unsure of himself, almost shy. If I did, I probably would've been on a motorcycle, headed south the day I turned eighteen. Who was I kidding? I was too much of a wuss to possess an ounce of spontaneity.

"Yeah, definitely." The answer came out without me giving it a single thought.

"Okay then. Let's just enjoy each other's company while we have it." He kissed me again. "I'm gonna head up to my room now, but I'll stop by the restaurant tomorrow. If that's alright with you?"

"Yeah, totally."

"Have a good night, Jonah." Micah waved as I watched him retreat inside the building. I vacantly stared through the glass doors until he disappeared around the corner of the lobby and out of view.

"What do you think, Sadie?" She barked, and I laughed. "That's my girl. I like him too, Ms. Sadie, probably far too much already." We jogged all the way home, getting our workout in. The house was quiet when we got inside, my parents having already gone to bed. I took the stairs two at a time with Sadie hot on my heels as we bounded into our room. I dropped back on the bed and wondered just what in the hell had I gotten myself into.

The pad of my fingertips trailed along the swollen flesh of my lips. How was it that I could still feel his mouth pressed to mine when he wasn't near? The rush I got from our kiss—*my first kiss*—ignited an insane four-alarm blaze that seared through me. Did it always feel this way, and I just didn't know? I mean, nearly twenty years old and kissed for the first time. *Wait.* Was it the other way around? No, I didn't... *Did I?* As I recalled the moment, I realized that I did kind of, sort of attack him. I didn't know what had possessed me, but as soon as the offer was on the table, it was like I couldn't continue the lifelong repression of—*everything*—and it rushed forth in a surge of electrified chaos. I had plowed into him, and he didn't gasp or back away when his backside hit the brick wall of the hotel. In fact, I felt his smile against my lips.

Maybe it wouldn't be so bad to have a summer fling? Just to break the seal, so to speak. I couldn't see myself turning into any sort of a playboy, especially considering it was the first time I had ever felt any sort of sexual energy. But why him? And why now? I guess that was the million-dollar question. All I knew was that I was about to become his summer boy and Micah would be mine.

I grabbed a pair of basketball shorts, toed off my shoes, and headed into the bathroom for a long, hot shower. My dick was still hard, suggesting I do something about its current situation. I had never so much as watched porn, never had the desire to do so. I could count the few times I jacked off on one hand, which was funny to think of, considering said hand was currently wrapped around said dick. Now I had all these thoughts and feelings, *urges*, when thinking of Micah. It was all just so...wow.

Those gray eyes, staring right into my soul.

*Ungh.*

I groaned with each stroke. What would it feel like to stroke Micah off?

*Ungh.* Our hands on each other's cocks.

*God. Yes.* That's what I wanted. I panted, stroking harder, faster.

"Fuck, Micah, make me come," I muttered aloud. "Yeah, just like that." The imagery of us together played through my mind as I came with a grunt and fell forward, the powerful orgasm nearly bringing me to my knees. The shower wall caught me and I leaned against it, welcoming the coolness on my warm skin, filled with a sense of hope that the real thing would be equally as intense. I finished washing, shut the shower off, and tumbled into bed still wrapped in a towel.

"Jonah, time for breakfast." My mother's voice wafted up the stairs the next morning, waking me from a deep slumber.

I groaned and ran my hand over my face. I was lucky in the sense that I never had to shave much, but at the same time, I had such a baby face that no one ever believed I was over the age of sixteen. Sort of a Catch-22. When young, you want to look older, and when older, you want to revert to being young again. *Go figure.* I rolled out of bed and pulled on a clean pair of jeans and one of my work polos, then walked across the hall to the bathroom. After brushing my teeth, I went downstairs to eat. Don't ask me why I brushed my teeth before eating. It was just something I'd always done, and I guess I was too lazy to change it.

"Morning, Jonah," Mom said.

"Morning, son," Dad followed.

"Morning," I grumbled in return. Again, just something we always did and they were more than aware I wasn't a morning person.

"How was your date last night?" Mom asked. Her words stopped me mid orange juice pour. Thankfully, I didn't drop the pitcher. My heart thudded against my chest, and my eyes nearly bugged out of my skull. I had never thought of it that way, as a *date*, until she said it.

"Oh, um...okay?"

She paused, flipping the pancakes. "Why do you sound so unsure?"

"I am. I mean, I'm not. I guess. I just didn't realize that it was a date until you said it."

She smiled. "So, it was just okay? Nothing great or earth-moving?"

"Actually, it was kind of great. We had a good time. Hung out at the bonfires. Sadie-girl got more pets and attention than she's had in her life." I glanced over at my sweet dog, her face buried in the dish as she ate her breakfast, tail wagging the entire time. *Crazy pup.* "He said he might come by the restaurant today. If we aren't busy, maybe we could hang out again?" I kind of, sort of asked.

"Help me stock everything and get through the lunch crowd and we'll see what we can do, son," my dad said. I expelled a rush of breath, not realizing I'd held it while anxiously awaiting their reactions. I'd never really asked for anything before and wasn't sure how they'd respond to any of these sudden changes. Hell, I didn't know how *I* would. I should have guessed my parents would still be cool about it, the whole me going on a date with a guy thing didn't appear to faze them.

Seems coming out, whether intentional or not, was un-eventful in the Thomas household.

Today was the first day of the Tall Ships Festival. Most of the visitors had arrived over the previous two days and the hotels were booked solid through Monday. There wasn't an empty parking spot to be found. I overheard Dad telling Mom that sales had already increased and he expected to see an even bigger influx today. Mom had hired a few locals to work shifts over the weekend. She and Dad kept a list of anyone willing to earn an extra buck whenever big events like this happened. They agreed to fill in all three days, so maybe I would get a reprieve in the form of time off. Though, when we rolled up the shutters covering the windows at opening, there was already an even bigger-than-usual line out front. That surprised me, given it was only eleven a.m.

"Welcome to Ahoy Matey's. How can I help you?" With those few simple words, the day was off and running.

I didn't have time to keep an eye out for Micah, let alone take a break to so much as go to the bathroom. The relentless line never ebbed. Dad and our backup cook, Mike, were flipping burgers like there was no tomorrow while Mom and I worked the prep station. Dakota and Justin manned the registers at the front service windows. There were four more employees scheduled to come in this afternoon and work until close, thank fuck. I was worn out. My fingers were crossed that they could handle it—the last thing I wanted was to have to come back and help out. Usually, the crowd died down after dark, when you couldn't see anything on the ships, though I had a feeling it wouldn't be doing much of that today. The second shift was going to probably be here late cleaning up, and Mom, Dad, and I would be coming in early to straighten up and stock everything, for sure.

"Is Jonah here?" My brain barely had time to register Micah's voice as he asked Justin where I was.

"Yeah, hey, I'm right here. Um, hold on a sec and I'll meet you out front." I wiped my hands off on my apron and glanced at Mom.

She nodded. "Go on, get out of here. You deserve a break. Go be a kid." I hung my apron on the hook, washed my hands, and met Micah near the side entrance.

"Wow you guys are crazy busy," Micah said, eyeing the never-ending line.

"It feels like this year's been busier than the last. What did you do today?"

Micah gestured to the line in front of us. "Same thing as the rest of the bodies crowding the town. Walked around a bunch of old ships, saw some cool shit, and, no lie, watched my sister geek out over some Jack Sparrow wannabe. Mostly, I thought about this gorgeous guy I met with curly blonde hair and killer blue eyes that mirror the sea."

My cheeks heated at his words. Compliments came so easily for Micah, but they weren't something I was accustomed to hearing. I needed to change the subject before my head exploded. "Do you or are you having dinner with your family tonight or what's the plan, I guess, is what I'm trying to ask."

Micah smiled. "The plan I was hoping to have involved you, me, possibly a cute chocolate lab named Sadie, and some alone time sans parental figures."

"What time can you escape yours?"

He sighed and leaned back. "I already did. My mom got tired of listening to me bitch while my sister ran from one exhibit to the next. I love my family, don't get me wrong, but I like them best in small doses."

"Alrighty then. Let me go check with my folks and see how things are going. Stay right here, okay?" Even to my own ears, I sounded frantic, like I was afraid he'd disappear into thin air.

Micah laughed at my exuberance. "I will. Go take care of whatever you need to. I'll be right here waiting." I watched as he pulled out his phone and started tapping the screen.

# CHAPTER SIX

**Micah**

D amn this guy was fucking adorable, and he had no clue he was. Everything about him called to me. Seeing how excited he got about spending time with me was like a breath of fresh air. I wasn't one to date, didn't have a significant other by choice. Never brought anyone home to meet the family, either. Nameless faces meant to scratch an itch with. I loved watching Jonah come out of his shell. Even though I'd only known him—what, two days?—I'd already noticed a big change. The way he took control last night with that kiss blew me away. Jonah was definitely not someone I'd soon forget, if ever.

It was odd not leading with my dick. Don't get me wrong, it was fully on board with my plans where Jonah was concerned. But sitting here and watching him work was oddly satisfying. I wasn't staring at the clock on my phone, counting down the minutes until we sealed the deal before getting back to homework or studying for midterms, preoccupied with what I had to do next. No, I was solely focused on the gorgeous man with whom I'd be spending all the time I could while in Stoney Brook. The lazy little town with a hidden gem I'd found.

*Shake out of it, Micah. You look like a freaking stalker.*

I groaned and switched to scrolling through my phone to occupy my time and fell down a black hole in the world of TikTok so much that I didn't hear Jonah walk up. "Whatcha watching?" Jonah asked, trying to get a glimpse of my screen.

I turned the phone toward him. "This guy has this cute pet spider monkey that he dresses up and carries around like a baby. Look, he wears a tiny diaper," I said, pointing to the screen. "The best part is how excited the monkey gets when he comes home from work." I shrugged, feeling a little stupid. I'd been following this guy since his inaugural post. "I have no idea why I'm so invested in this, outside of it making me smile at times when smiles are hard to come by."

"Ha! He uses one of those baby carriers that goes across your chest to carry him in. That is so freaking cute." Jonah chuckled and my heart grew ten sizes. The so-called friends I had at home thought I was ridiculous, following all the animal rescuers that I did, yet Jonah enjoyed it. This guy suited me in so many ways, it was scary. Everything I wanted but never knew I needed.

"Animals are amazing. It's sad most humans don't understand how closely related they are to us. They feel what we feel—same anxieties, same medical issues, same mostly everything," Jonah continued.

"Exactly. Leave me outside all night, tied up or otherwise, and I'd be terrified and barking too."

"I couldn't imagine doing that to Sadie. I don't even let her out to pee alone. She's my best friend and confidant. No one gets me like she does," Jonah added.

Every word in the English language left my brain at his declaration, the love for his dog shining through. It was, like, he got me and he didn't even know it.

"Are you alright?" Jonah asked. Between his acknowledgment of Sadie's importance to him and his show of concern for me, nearly a complete stranger, I gasped for breath, overwhelmed at how easily this beautiful, shy soul had opened up to me. Breaking through the reticence that I knew he had was heavy and said so much about how comfortable he was with me. And I liked being that person for him.

I tripped over my own feet and grumbled. I really needed to get out of my own head. I shook it off, mentally berating myself for being such a dumbass. "Um, yeah. Just need to watch where I'm going." I needed to lighten the mood. "So, what's on the agenda for tonight?"

"Well," Jonah began, "you've seen the whole town, all ten minutes of it, so now you know why I bury myself in video games. There's not much else to do. I go fishing with my dad sometimes, but when it gets too cold out, there's no fishing to be had unless you count ice fishing. And we can only do that in the lagoon, so we don't do much of that. I don't know, do you like video games?"

"Does chocolate melt in the sun?" I teased.

"Huh?"

"I was being a smartass, Jonah. Yes, I like video games and by the way, chocolate does melt in the sun."

"Good to know. Guess I need to get used to your sense of humor," he said. "I mean," Jonah blushed, "at least while you're here."

We made the short walk up the hill to Jonah's house. It was at the opposite end of town from where the hotel was, each hill nearly mirroring the other. The hotel's and the one with Jonah's home, along with the rest along the crest between the two, framed the quaint village, presenting the viewer with an idyllic Norman Rockwell painting.

The inside of his house was comfortable, a picture-perfect 1970s cabin. Avocado appliances, wall-to-wall carpeting, wood walls. It was dated, although clean, yet warm and inviting. Though I was raised in a different demographic than Jonah, I didn't feel out of place here. There were certain things in our house you didn't touch, they were for guests only, whereas here, everyone was made to feel welcome.

"Kitchen." He pointed to the left as we walked in. Then a big grin spread across his face when his dog came bounding toward us. "Sadie girl," he cooed as she sat at his feet. We lavished her with pets and she rolled over so her belly could join the mix, clearly enjoying the scritches. "Come on, girl, time to go out."

I followed Jonah and Sadie outside. "Wow, this view is epic," I said, taking it in. Water as far as the eye could see.

"Yeah, my parents like to sit out here after work and unwind. We had to put up the fence after Sadie joined the family. She came far too close to cliff-diving one too many times for me."

"Oh, shit. Glad you did."

"You and me both. This girl right here is my world," Jonah said, hugging his pretty gal.

When Sadie was done, we went back inside and headed upstairs, Sadie hot on our heels. "This is my room. Not much, but it's my sanctuary."

"I think it's cool. It's like a studio apartment." He had a sweet setup. I think at some point his room had been an attic that was then converted. It was huge, basically ran the entire length of the house. He had it sectioned off into separate areas. On one side was his sleeping area with a bed and nightstand, while another area posed as a living room with a couch and wall unit. The bathroom door was open, and I peeked inside as we walked past. In the far corner was another door I assumed was the closet.

He plopped down on the couch and turned on his TV. "Halo, Call of Duty? Or is Mario Kart more your style?" He reached over, snagging a bucket off a nearby shelf, and handed it to me as I took the seat beside him. It was filled with a variety of games.

"How many systems do you have?" Holy crap, this thing was filled to the brim.

He shrugged. "Don't know. Four? Five? I have some vintage systems and those games are mixed in there with the PlayStation 4 and Xbox ones. We can set any of them up that you want. They're over there." He gestured to a cabinet door at the bottom of the wall unit that also housed the TV.

"You have quite the collection, Jonah. I didn't see a game shop or major retailer in town. How do you get a hold of these?" I said, trying to decide what to play. Which was least likely to get my ass handed to me while playing? That would be none!

"It passes the time. The winters are long and boring here. Augusta is about two hours away, so once a month my parents and I take a trip over, pick up things we need. They drop me off at the mall and I do my thing while they do theirs."

"It's been a while since I've played Mario Kart. Like, sophomore year, to be honest. I used to love it, but I'm sure I'm rusty. Let's load that one up. Best two of three?" I suggested, figuring this would give me time to get warmed up and to get a feel for my competitor.

"What does the winner get?" Jonah asked.

"What's on the table?" I returned, interested to see what he'd offer.

"I don't know. I always play online against other people. We virtually torment the losers, talk shit. It's kinda fun." He smirked. Seemed shy Jonah had an ornery side. I had a feeling he would be a formidable opponent given the amount of time it sounded like he spent playing.

"Okay, then." I took a minute to think. Initially, I thought a kiss would be a good ante but now I felt the need to up the stakes. "Winner gets to..." I froze as his intense gaze locked on mine. I didn't know what it was about this guy, but he had the ability to render me speechless. I licked my lips, swallowed, and tried again. "Better yet, loser blows the winner." I had a gut feeling Jonah hadn't done that before and had already resigned myself to being the loser. Plus, I was dying to get a taste of him.

Jonah stared at me, his face a kaleidoscope of reds. Would he run? Would he kick me out? I waited for what felt like forever for his response.

He surprised me when he smiled and said, "Game on."

"You have a great smile," I replied. He blushed again. Or, more like, reignited the shades his face had already spiraled through.

Jonah tossed a spare controller in my lap. "Pick your character, player."

*Player?* Was that what he thought of me? Sure, in the reality that was my life, I was. But with Jonah, I wasn't. I wanted to make this guy happy in any way I could and for the life of me, I couldn't explain why.

Turned out I was even rustier than I thought. Jonah kicked my ass all three games. He stared blankly down at his controller after his Luigi character was awarded the trophy. My guts lurched, maybe I pushed too much too fast with the blowjob offer. "Are you okay?" I asked him, readying to rescind the bet.

"Yeah, just, um..." He tossed the controller down and drew a deep breath. "I've never done this."

I gathered that, given last night's kiss. Was it selfish of me to make this bet, assuming that ahead of time? "We don't have to do it if you don't want to." "Oh, it's not that I don't want to. Trust me, I do. It's that I know I'm gonna blow as soon as your mouth gets anywhere near my dick." He ducked his head and grinned. Oh, this guy wasn't as shy as I thought, either that or he was more than ready to pop his proverbial cherry.

Now that I knew he didn't feel pressured, it was time to pay up. "That's a chance I'm willing to take." I sat the controller down, dropped to my knees, scooted across the carpet, and stopped in front of him. I nudged his legs apart and crawled up between them.

"Are you sure you're okay with this?" Jonah bobbed his head in response. I leaned in and kissed him, hoping to ease his nerves. When our lips met, things quickly escalated. It was like neither of us had any control as we consumed each other.

I finally broke away and pressed my lips to the skin beneath his ear, whispering, "If you want me to stop at any time, just say the word. You're the one in control here, Jonah." It was important he understood this. I thought he was into me, but I could be reading it all wrong, or he could totally freak out once it started. Maybe he was just into the blowjob itself. Being demisexual, his interests may not be in sync with mine. I was okay with being an experiment for Jonah, so to speak, in his pursuit to find himself.

I returned my lips to his as I reached down and teased his cock through his jeans. Jonah's lips parted and he released an audible gasp as he dropped his head back. Hastily, I unbuttoned his pants and slid the zipper down. His boxers had a dark spot where precome had dampened them. I leaned down to run my tongue over the area and Jonah hissed. The need to taste more overwhelmed my senses. I tugged at his waistband, and he lifted enough to allow me to slide his pants and boxers down. With his cock free, I took it in hand and gave it a couple of rough strokes. When he still didn't react, I whispered his name to get his attention. "Jonah?"

"Yeah?"

"Please look at me." Reluctantly, he glanced down. "I want you to watch me." Without breaking eye contact, I ran my tongue along the underside of his shaft. Reaching the head, I drew it inside.

"Oh God," Jonah whispered, which goaded me on. His hips thrust up, forcing his cock to hit the back of my throat and I gagged. "Shit, I'm sorry," he apologized.

"Don't be. I like it rough. I just wasn't expecting it." I put his hand on my head and moved my mouth back in place, then guided his movement so he would catch on. He was still uncertain, and I understood why, but I refused to let that affect my performance. He'd figure it out on his own. While it was hard for a blowjob to be bad, as long as you kept teeth out of it, I'd fixated on making this a positive memory for him in every way possible.

I could tell that Jonah neared the edge quickly, just as he'd anticipated, when his movements became frantic. He was ready to blow.

"Ohfuckohfuckohfuck!" was the only warning I got before Jonah came. I swallowed it down, lapping at the head as he rode out the aftershocks.

"I'm so sorry," he apologized again, once he'd come down from the euphoric high.

"What for?"

"I. Um." Embarrassed, he pointed at my mouth. "You know."

"So, you're old enough to come but not old enough to say the word itself?" I teased.

"Wasn't I supposed to warn you so you could pull off or something?"

I shrugged. "Generally, a warning would be nice. But I wouldn't have pulled off even if you had."

"Oh. Why?"

I flashed him a shit-eating grin. "Because I fully intended to swallow every last drop." I pulled his pants up, tucked his dick away, and popped back into the seat beside him, then grabbed his controller and started up a new game before handing it back to him like nothing had happened. I didn't want to make this any more awkward for him than it already seemed to be. We were mid-game when his parents came home.

"Jonah?" His mom hollered up the stairs.

"Coming," he called back.

"See, that wasn't so hard to say now, was it?" It took him a minute to get it. When he did, he shook his head and laughed.

"Wanna sleep over?" He asked as he crossed the room to go see what his mom wanted.

Surprised, I asked, "Your parents would be okay with that?"

"Probably. But I won't know for sure until I ask," Jonah replied.

"Have you ever had anybody sleep over?" It wouldn't surprise me if this was another first for him.

"Nope. Is that bad?" Jonah asked, pausing with his hand on the rail as he patiently awaited my response.

"No, just surprised is all. My friends and I used to sleep over at each other's houses almost every weekend before we went to college. Now we just crash out—well, more like pass out—at whoever's dorm we'd landed in that night. Your parents would be cool with a twenty-year-old sleeping over?" Why I kept pushing with these stupid questions was beyond me, and I seemed to be the only one fixated on our ages. I wanted to smack myself, yet the questions just kept coming.

"They have a son pretty much the same age, so why wouldn't they be okay with it?" Jonah replied.

"Okay, sounds good to me. Let me text my parents. Let them know what's up so they don't worry." He nodded and proceeded down the stairs. I was excited about spending more time with Jonah but had to mentally berate myself to slow my roll and let him take the lead. One thing I didn't want to do was scare him off.

# CHAPTER SEVEN

**Jonah**

"Hey, Mom," I said when I'd reached the kitchen. "How were the lines out front when you guys left?"

She sighed and plopped down in the kitchen chair. "I'm beat. It was nonstop, but the crew coming in felt that they could handle it and shooed us out. I told them to call if they needed anything. Hopefully, they won't. I'm sure tomorrow will be equally as insane, if not more so. Is your friend still here?"

"Yeah, he's upstairs."

She stood. "Well, I'll get to making us some dinner then."

"No, don't worry about it. Just take care of you and Dad, we'll get food later. We're playing games right now anyway. Um, would it be cool if he spent the night?" I asked, nervously rubbing my hands together.

She turned to my dad, who simply shrugged. "Not like anybody's gonna get pregnant."

*Oh. My. God.*

I wanted to fucking die. I stood there, unable to move, my face on fire. I visualized myself looking like that character from *Inside Out*, Anger, with flames shooting out of the top of my head, mirroring his. Dad laughed and Mom shook her head at him. "Yes, son, that's fine. Holler if you two need anything. Otherwise, I'll let you take care of yourselves."

"Thanks, Mom." I ran back upstairs. I couldn't get away fast enough, beyond shocked my dad said that.

"Everything alright?" Micah asked. "Your face is flushed."

"Yeah, it's nothing." Sharing Dad's words with Micah wasn't gonna happen. I'd probably drop dead of embarrassment on the spot. "My parents said it's cool if you stayed. I told them we'd get something to eat later. Unless you're hungry now?" I asked. Probably shouldn't have spoken for him.

"Nah, man, I'm good with getting something later. Wanna switch to Halo?" Micah suggested.

"Sounds like a plan." I figured it'd be another game I'd kick his ass at and wondered if he'd be open to another wager. Maybe this awakening I was experiencing with Micah was more like opening Pandora's Box.

Micah wasn't any better at Halo than he was at Mario Kart. I wasn't sure if he was only playing to humor me or if he really was good at them at one time.

He grumbled and tossed the controller aside after losing again. "Dude, I'm dragging down your online rankings."

"Nah, don't worry about it. It's all good, they're just games. Do you wanna do something else?" I could tell he was done with this.

"Is anything open in town?"

I looked at the clock on the wall. "Yeah, it's only about seven o'clock. On a Friday night? Most of the restaurants should still be open, but they are probably packed with festival visitors. You wanna go take a look, just in case?"

"I could go for a pizza. I remember passing a place over on Main Street."

"Crazy Jim's. It's really good." My stomach chose that moment to rumble in agreement. "Seems my body has decided it's food time after all."

"Sounds good." Micah stood, brushing off the front of his pants. Probably got covered with Sadie's hair.

"Alright, cool." I shut everything down before we went downstairs, where we walked in on Mom and Dad just sitting down to eat. "We're gonna head into town, probably grab a pizza. Oh, man, I forgot to introduce you. Mom, Dad, this is Micah. Micah, these are my parents, Joan and Michael."

"Nice to meet you Mr. and Mrs....?" He paused, staring at me.

"Uh, Thomas," I filled in. Dad snickered and Mom dipped her head, likely doing the same.

Micah shook their hands. "Nice to meet you."

"You too, Micah. Glad to see Jonah's got a friend to get out of the house with for a little while."

"Dad, you're on a roll tonight," I tossed back, having been the brunt of two *friend* jokes since they got home.

"Yes, son, I've got all the jokes. Don't I?" Dad teased. He was clearly enjoying himself, though, which made it hard to be mad at him.

"You got something, alright," Mom said, patting his hand. Dad smiled lovingly back at her. It struck me then how great it would be to have that connection with some-one. We should all be so lucky to snag the love of our life when we're kids like my parents did.

"Alright, we're gonna head out. I'll be back later. I already fed Sadie and took her out, so she's good to go." Micah and I told Sadie goodbye, patting her head as we left.

We were halfway down the driveway when Micah took my hand in his. "Is this still okay?" he asked.

"Yeah."

Inside my excitement was on a higher level than the one-word responses I gave him. I was trying to play it cool though. I loved the attention he gave me. Without a doubt, this would be more than a summer fling for me, but that was my burden to bear, not his. Already, I could feel the pieces of my heart getting stamped with bright red *M's* as they filled with Micah. He was winning me over and far too fast. It was gonna be hard for me when he left, but I was determined to enjoy every minute with him that I could.

When we stepped inside Jim's, my eyes immediately scanned the packed place.

"Hey, Jonah. I haven't seen you in here for a while. How are your mom and dad?" Jim asked as we reached the front of the line.

"They're good, at home relaxing. It was a crazy busy day," I replied.

"Tell me about it."

He was swamped, too, and yet he still had a smile on his face and a friendly word for everyone who approached him. "This is my friend, Micah. He's in town with his family for the festival."

"Alright, Micah-who's-in-town. Nice to meet you," Jim teased. "What can I get for you two?"

We ordered the daily special, which was a large one-topping pizza and two drinks. Jim handed us our cups and the number to place on the table, then we had to stand off to the side and wait for a seat. As soon as a table cleared, Micah ran over and grabbed it while I filled our drinks.

"Wow, this place is hopping," Micah said as I handed him his cup.

"Jim does pretty well year-round. He's one of the few places that stays open during the winter. He's been known to make deliveries via snowmobile when the snow gets too high to drive in. No other choice because everyone is stuck inside." Man, what I wouldn't give to live in a town that never shut down. Especially not due to weather. Year-round sunshine was more my style. Hopefully, I'd have that someday soon. "Jim's a bit of an overachiever."

"I couldn't imagine being stuck inside for days on end. I'd go freaking nuts. I was born and raised in Florida. It'd take an act of God to shut that state down," Micah replied, gazing around the overly crowded room.

"My parents want to retire and move to Florida," I said, nervously fidgeting with the straw wrapper. I wasn't sure why I was so wound up. "Honestly, I'm not sure why they picked that state. I hope we do get to move, though. I don't hate it here, but it's not really where I want to be. Shoveling snow is not my idea of a good time. Being trapped all winter long, I go stir crazy."

"I totally would too. I love the outdoors, and like I said before, anything and everything to do with playing in the water is for me," Micah replied, taking a sip of his drink.

I chuckled softly. "You're like a human Labrador retriever. I get it, I feel the same way. I don't know, it just seems like life outside of Stoney Brook would be more fulfilling, like I'm missing out on so much living here." I sighed. The reality of my words was far *too* real and I was bringing this date down. "Who knows, maybe once I get out of this place, the path I'm meant to follow will appear. For now, I feel trapped both mentally and physically, and my psyche can't get past that. There's nothing here that interests me. Don't get me wrong, it's not a bad place. Just the opposite."

"Stoney Brook is Americana at its finest, as far as I can tell," Micah said.

"It's a great place to raise a family. We have zero crime, at least that I'm aware of. I don't know if that makes any sense? Maybe I'm just crazy. It's like I said before, one thing I know for sure is that I definitely do not want to run Ahoy Matey's. I don't even know if I want to run *any* business. Maybe I'm just meant for nothing more than a mundane, meaningless existence." Great, now I'd depressed the fuck out of myself. *Way to kill the mood, Jonah.*

"I disagree. What is it they say? 'The world is at your fingertips, you just need to find the right finger and not the middle one.'" Micah smiled. "I don't know why you keep putting yourself down. Like I told you before, not everybody finds their path in life at the age of eighteen, nor should we be forced to. I hate that society and our parents pressure us, but nobody is inside our heads. They have no freaking clue what's going on in there. Not everyone is the same. In fact, nobody is, and we shouldn't be treated like cookie-cutter humans."

"You're right." I tossed the wadded-up paper I'd been messing with onto the table. "I think I just need to get out of here. I feel like I'm gonna go crazy if I don't." Shit, Micah probably already thought I was destined for a padded cell.

Our pizza came a few minutes later, and I was extremely thankful for the distraction. The first bite Micah took, he released a salacious moan that shot straight to my cock. I didn't know what to think. It was like I went from zero to sixty where Micah was concerned and I couldn't wrap my head around it. No pun intended. I was nowhere near as experienced as he was, yet I knew that if the opportunity presented itself, I'd let Micah be my first. He'd already been for so many things already, though I hadn't shared that with him. I'm sure my fumbling around had him figuring it out on his own though.

I wasn't sure what to expect or, more accurately, what Micah would expect when we crawled into my bed together once we got home. Micah must've sensed my nerves, though, because he seemed okay with it when we rolled to face each other and talked until we could no longer hold our eyes open, then woke with our limbs round around one another. It was...heaven even without anything sexual taking place. We gave each other what we needed, which was beyond that.

# CHAPTER EIGHT

**Micah**

E very day at five p.m., my internal time clock—a recent development—sounded and led me to Jonah. It took all I had not to plant myself at one of Ahoy Matey's benches and watch him work throughout the day. I'd only be a selfish distraction for him if I did that, which wasn't fair. Which, honestly, was the only reason I didn't do it. I'd never craved another human the way I did Jonah and to be honest, it scared the shit out of me. Needy wasn't something I cared to be, and I was struggling with this new side of me. Was it fair of me to pursue this with Jonah? Likely not, but I couldn't bring myself to stop.

I understood what he meant about feeling trapped. I could see that. As an outsider looking in, Stoney Brook was a great place to raise a family, appearing to be tucked away inside a bubble all its own, untouched by the evils of the outside world—though, as I walked along, I passed more humans than I had in a long time. Each of us invading the local residents' personal space. Great, now I felt like some sort of evil warlord.

The water views were so different than those back home. Wall-to-wall beach bodies, towels, and umbrellas covered the sands of Florida, yet Stoney Brook had their own version of sandy areas, ones that, though minimal in comparison, seemed virtually untouched. Even with as many people as there were here right now, it had a different look and feel than what I was used to. For one thing, trash wasn't in need of being picked up. Here were responsible adults who did as they should and made certain their trash was placed in the proper receptacles. The water in the lagoon was crystal clear, and the only fear of going barefoot was the chance of slicing your foot on a piece of shell, rather than broken glass, and leaving it scarred. I had also yet to see a palm tree, which was a welcome change.

*Scars.*

Some run deeper than others. Would Jonah scar my heart? Could the reality be that I was falling fast and hard for someone? It was bound to happen at some point in my life, but why did it have to be someone I couldn't keep? Fourteen hundred miles separated us. The fates can be an evil fucking bitch. I drew in a sharp, knowing breath as I neared the restaurant. My eyes were immediately drawn to Jonah, and his did the same to me. I froze as our gazes met. My heart pounded as I neared, though I had no idea what was going on. But it appeared that I wasn't alone. Seemed neither of us was walking away from this brief romance unscathed.

Jonah nodded, then turned and spoke to his mother while I stood rooted in place. Soon enough, he was in front of me, his adorable face flushed. Without thinking, I reached out to pull him into my arms, then pressed my lips to his.

I felt...whole.

He flinched and pulled back. It took me a minute before my brain registered what I had done. Not only were we in the middle of a packed area, but I'd just outed him. This was more than just hand-holding, and I'd let my feelings and needs take control, which was the worst thing I could've done. Fuck, I was such an asshole.

"Shit." I dropped my arms quickly. "I'm so sorry. I didn't—I didn't think."

He fidgeted and shoved his hands in his pockets. "Don't think I didn't enjoy it. I did. Just would've preferred we weren't entertaining a crowd." He glanced at the front of the building, catching his mother's eye as she waved at us. "Or my parents."

Fuck. I felt like such a fool.

"Come on, let's go," Jonah said, walking ahead of me and off into the wooded area beside his house.

Not a word was spoken between us as I followed him along a trail that ended up winding down around a steep embankment behind where he lived. The only sound was the crunching of leaves and pine needles beneath our feet.

"Wow," I said, stopping at a clearing in the small forest to take in the change in view.

"Almost there," Jonah replied as he continued down the path.

The terrain changed from solid to rocky as we exited the canopy. Carefully, we climbed over the rock formations along the waterfront. I could easily see why this area wasn't populated with families. Getting here wasn't the safest, and there wasn't any flat ground or sandy area for them to sit on and enjoy the water.

"I get that I just outed you in front of what appeared to be the entire town, but offing me in a remote area where my body would never be found feels a bit harsh," I half-ass joked, fearing Jonah may be mad enough to leave my sorry ass here. Without answering, he disappeared around a ginormous boulder, scaring the hell out of me.

"Jonah!" I called out, trying to get to him. "Whoa," I said, only to freeze where I was as the breathtaking view came into my line of sight.

The other side was nothing to balk at. It was a hidden cave with a sandy base, rocks on three sides keeping it from discovery. Needless to say, Jonah was safe and currently laying out a blanket he must've kept stashed there. "This is seriously cool."

Jonah shrugged. "Yeah, it's like a secret hideaway."

"Have you ever camped out here overnight?"

"No, I'd be trapped when high tide rolled in."

"True. Look, Jonah," I said, taking a seat beside him, "I really am so sorry I outed you. I broke the cardinal rule, and you have every right to hate me."

He picked up a shell, turning it over in his hand. "I don't know much about that. All of this is just new to me and still feels private, you know?" Jonah turned toward me and those gorgeous eyes locked on mine. "You're only here for a little while, but I'm here until my parents decide what they want to do. And I'm already wrapped up in you." He blushed and turned away. "It's gonna suck when you leave."

That I got. Heavy doses of the blues had smacked me earlier over this exact same thing. "That I more than understand."

"You do?" Jonah asked, seemingly surprised. Did he not realize I was vested in this too?

I took his hand in mine. "I do. Jonah, I don't know how or why, but you got to me, and I can't seem to shake you. Not that I want to or even tried, but there you go."

In an instant, he was on me, knocking me backward and pinning me beneath him. He stared down at me, smirking. "Hi."

"Hi."

"Is this okay?" he asked, chewing his bottom lip.

"More than." No truer words had ever come from my mouth.

This time when Jonah's lips met mine, it was like my world righted. Like everything wrong and missing in my life, all the voids, were fixed, filled in by this amazing guy on top of me.

His kisses were tentative, repeated small pecks. I held back, letting him lead. I wanted more, but he needed to initiate what happened next so I was leaving it in Jonah's hands. After taking charge as I had in his room, then outing him, I didn't want to risk fucking up again. Third time might not be a charm in this situation.

Jonah rolled us over, our mouths still firmly pressed together. Body to body, groin to groin, and it was driving me up the freaking wall. "Jonah," I panted, "need more."

"Show me," Jonah replied.

I reached for the button of his jeans. "May I?" He nodded. Slowly, I undid his pants and freed his cock, then did the same with mine. I wrapped my fist around both and stroked. Jonah gasped, mouth open and head back. I couldn't help but kiss the exposed flesh of his neck. "Tell me what you want, Jonah," I seductively whispered.

"This. This is...God. Feels so good," he moaned.

Two fast strokes, one slow. With every repeat of the sequence, Jonah emitted a new sound, each more sensual than the last. I openly stared, unable to take my eyes off him, filled with a need to unravel him, one strand at a time. I increased the strokes. Driven with a desire to watch him come, to see this beautiful man fall apart in the throes of passion. Knowing the sight would draw forth my own, and I fucking needed that badly. I was somewhere between pain and pleasure, right on the precipice, but I needed him to come first.

"Jonah, baby. Come for me," I whispered.

Baby? When had I ever uttered that word? No, now was not the time to dissect that, not when my balls were crawling inside my body, screaming for release.

He drew in his bottom lip, fucked up into my first, and succumbed to the need his body so desperately sought. He was fucking beautiful when he came. Bearing witness to this amazing transformation pushed me over the edge, and my warm come joined his. I fell back onto my haunches, panting, mirroring Jonah's sated expression.

"Whoa," Jonah muttered.

"Whoa is right," I said as I committed to memory the earth-moving scenario that had just played out. Addicted? Yes, please!

The sun was setting as we straightened up. Jonah stashed the blanket back where he kept it stored while I climbed my way over to the water and washed off. Though we were once again silent during the walk back, we did so while holding hands. A completely different feel than the trip down had been and I couldn't have been happier. My fuck up was no longer at the forefront, but thoughts of more, wanting more with Jonah, filled my mind.

"Want to hang out in my room for a while?" Jonah asked as we reached the end of the path, next to his house.

"Yeah, sounds good."

We stopped to say hi to his parents as we passed through the kitchen to grab two sodas from the fridge before heading upstairs.

"Games again?" Jonah asked.

I was looking through his DVD collection. "How about a movie fest?"

"What are you in the mood for?"

Now there was a loaded question. I nearly responded, "*You*." Even though I'd just had him, it wasn't enough. For now, I decided to keep it light and stick with the movie theme.

"How about a Resident Evil marathon?"

"Sounds good to me." Jonah reached out and snagged the DVD for the first movie, then loaded it up. We sat on the couch, a couple of inches separating us. Barely any time had passed since we got off in the cave, yet I felt the urge to reach out and pull him against me, do it all over again. Instead, I scooted closer, resting my head on his shoulder and my hand on his thigh. This right here, cuddling, soothed my mind.

# CHAPTER NINE

**Jonah**

*W*hat is the etiquette for this?

I stared down at his hand resting on my thigh, so many questions running through my brain. I didn't know how to begin asking or if I should say anything at all.

*Should I just enjoy whatever Micah offers while he's here? Maybe we start making out like I heard guys talk about do-*

*ing after they would go to the movies with their girlfriends?*
This was sorta like that.

I remembered talk of first and second base, but if my
perceptions of what the bases consisted of were correct, all
Micah and I missed was a home run. An easily obtainable
goal, one that could be reached in my room. Alone. No
rules. My parents wouldn't come up here unannounced,
they weren't wired like that. Plus, they knew Micah was
here. My arms were itching to hold him. My hands shook
with a need to touch him, pull him close, never let him go.
Sadly, in a couple of days, that option would be taken from
me.

"The Tall Ship Festival ends tomorrow," Micah said. I
wondered if he was somehow inside my head.

"Yeah, things should calm down by Tuesday. Most people leave on Monday," I replied.

"We leave on Friday, but my parents wanted to drive
around and do some sightseeing between now and then,
while we were still in Maine," Micah said, staring every-
where but at me.

"Oh." That hit like a kick to the gut. I'd become used to
spending my evenings after work with Micah. I knew that
was selfish of me. After all, he was here with his family but
had already spent a lot of his vacation with me. "Are you
coming back to Stoney Brook at night, or are you staying

in other towns?" Even to my own ears, I sounded greedy, which I didn't mean to be.

"My parents have the hotel here booked through Thursday night, so if they have any other plans, they haven't said. They want to get home on Saturday so Mom has Sunday to get things sorted before she and Dad go back to work on Monday," Micah replied.

I'd had friends come and go when I was in grade school. Some had parents who would get job transfers and they'd move, others got divorced and the family members would go their separate ways. None of that had ever hit me as hard as knowing that my days with Micah were coming to an end.

I didn't understand why I had such strong feelings for him. I had read up on demisexuality, and while I understood it and could see myself defined within that label, it still didn't fully explain the range of emotions I was going through. How could I be this drawn to one person this quickly? Why did the thought of him leaving fucking crush me? I mean, above all else, why did I feel anything at all toward him? Would I always be sad after he was gone or would I be able to work past it? Then there's the other side of that coin, where I wondered if I was merely being foolish, leading with my heart. I was no closer to having any answers now than I was pre-Micah, when I had still believed I was broken. I wanted to ask him more about it, about being demi, because he seemed to understand it better than I did, though I also didn't want to play the role of the small-town fool by doing so. *Should I tell him, or will I just look like a total dumbass?* If we were in an actual relationship, I probably would, but knowing what this was, I figured it may be best to keep my feelings locked away.

Summer romance is not for those who are led by their heart.

"What are you thinking so hard about over there?" Micah asked.

I shrugged. It seemed to be my go-to reply as of late. Clearing my throat, I finally managed a reply. "I don't know, just thinking about stuff."

"What kind of stuff?" Micah shifted on the couch to face me and raised my chin with one finger, putting us eye-to-eye. "Talk to me, Jonah."

I took a deep breath, steeled my nerves, and decided to bare it all. "I guess I'm struggling to understand all of this. My sexuality, amongst other things. I don't get why I'm not only attracted to you but that it also feels like such a soul-deep bond. It sounds stupid when I say it out loud, doesn't it? I don't know, I can't explain it right, I guess."

Micah surprised me when he replied, "You're not alone in this, Jonah."

"What do you mean?"

"I'm feeling it, too, and trust me, I'm not any more familiar with what's going on than you are. It's making things extremely difficult, knowing it will be coming to an end far too soon. I wish we didn't live so far apart and could build an actual relationship. I've come to care a lot for you, Jonah. Leaving isn't going to be easy." Micah leaned in and kissed me.

When our lips parted, I blurted out, "Is it dumb that I wish you didn't have to go?"

"I don't know. Is it dumb that I wish I didn't have to either?"

I couldn't help but smile when he called me out on it, answering my question with one of his own, forcing us to laugh. "Okay, guess we're both being dumb, then. Good to know."

We returned to watching the movie, and right as it ended, his phone rang. "Hey, Dad, what's up? Yeah, that's fine. I'll be there soon. Alright, bye." Micah hung up. "My dad asked if I'd be back at the hotel tonight. I guess someone told him about another town nearby. Something about pies. I don't know, but they want to check it out. Now, instead of going to the festival tomorrow, we're going there."

I didn't know what to say. Did I scream *no, you're mine, you're staying here with me,* or was that too stalkerish? I wasn't sure my parents would want the family on the ten o'clock news, and the idea of taking away Micah's free will by chaining him to me would be doing just that, which was wrong on more levels than I could count.

"I'll come by as soon as we get back tomorrow, if that's okay with you. If it's late, can I still come by, just meet you here instead?" Micah asked. Like I'd even say no. I knew I'd wait up all night for him.

"Yeah, of course. I'll be here," I assured him.

"Alright. I better head back to the hotel then." Micah stood and stretched, his shirt rising just enough to give me a glimpse of the skin I longed to touch. I walked him to the door where he kissed me goodbye and watched as he headed down the hill and out of sight, lost to the darkness of night.

I was quiet the next morning at breakfast, and thankful that my parents didn't question it. How would I explain that I was falling in love with someone I hardly knew? Someone I couldn't have. With it being the last day of the festival, we were ridiculously swamped, which still didn't stop me from looking out the window a million times, hoping to catch a glimpse of Micah standing nearby. He never came, nor did he show up later that night. It wasn't until Monday afternoon when I saw him again, standing in his usual spot, waiting for me.

"Jonah, I'm sorry about last night. My parents decided to stay the night where we were. I tried to convince them we weren't that far away, I even offered to drive back so they could rest. It was so stupid, we were only in the next town over, but I was trapped with them. I hate not having my own vehicle with me," Micah apologized though he didn't need to.

"I understand, and you don't owe me any apology. I mean, it's not like you knew what they had planned, nor is it my place to take you away from your family. I get it," I assured him. And I did get it, but I wasn't about to tell him how bad it sucked being apart, and how I was running on fumes after waiting up all night for him. Guilt trips weren't my thing.

"Still, it was rude and I'm sorry. Are you free tonight?" Micah asked, and the butterflies in my stomach shot off like rockets.

I laughed. "You know I am. I have no life."

"Don't look now," Micah said, "but that girl from the next shift is eye-fucking you."

"Yeah, well, she's got problems." And I wasn't going to be the one to fix them.

Micah laughed and took my hand with a flourish, making a show of it. The feeling of being claimed nearly had me dancing as we walked away. "What do you say we go get Sadie and take her for a walk?" Micah suggested. I was totally on board with that plan and loved how he included my girl.

When we got to my house, I snagged the leash off the hook while Sadie excitedly greeted Micah. Seemed I was second best when he was around, not that I minded.

"I see how you work, little girl," I told her when she finally realized I was in the room. She barked. "Don't worry, Sadie, I like him too." As we walked along, we noticed that the town was mostly cleared out, something I had expected when I saw the number of visitors hitting the road this morning. Still, a handful lingered. Business had been steady today, but nowhere near as insane as the last few days. Dad and I even had managed to find the time to restock and take inventory so he could place a new supply order.

The visitors along the waterfront were few and far between. The bonfires had been deconstructed, and things were returning to the status quo, back to the normal Stoney Brook life I was used to.

But this season I had changed. I knew, once Micah left, that I had to get a grip on who the real Jonah Thomas was, having discovered so much about myself because of him. Ultimately, I was the only one who could control my destiny. I knew I wanted to start my new life in Florida, now more than ever. And if my parents weren't going to move, I was going to have to figure out how to do it on my own.

"Jonah, do you think you could get Thursday off?" Micah asked, putting my brain meanderings on hold. "It's my last night here."

I sighed. "We've got a big order coming in that day. Maybe after I help my dad unload and get it put away, I could take off?"

"Or maybe I could help you guys with it and then you can get done faster and we'd have more time together." Micah proudly smirked, wagging his brows at me.

It felt good having someone around who wanted to spend this much time with me, but by the same token, it made it that much harder to let him go. But I wouldn't give up what Micah and I had shared for the world. I knew I would just have to deal with whatever pain came from losing him once he left.

Micah spent the night again. What started off as a simple exploration of flesh—kissing, touching, learning what made the other tick in the best of ways—had every fiber of my body ignited. This was the first time I touched another person intimately, and up until this point it had always been Micah doing most of the work because I worried I'd do something wrong. It wasn't fair to him that I didn't reciprocate, and it wasn't that I didn't want to but more that I didn't know how.

"Relax, Jonah," Micah whispered. "Do what comes naturally, whatever you enjoy. It'll likely feel the same way for me."

Micah had a point. What did it matter whose cock it was? A cock was a cock. You just learned what your partners liked as you went along. It wasn't rocket science, or dick science in this case, and I was wasting precious time dwelling on it. Gently nipping the sensitive area below my ear, Micah drew me from my fears, out of my own head, and back to the present, where I needed to be. With him.

Kissing, stroking, panting, it didn't take long before we tumbled over the edge. Sated, sweaty, and beyond tired, we fell asleep shortly after sharing mutual hand jobs.

Every day, Micah would show up at the restaurant at five, then come home with me and spend the night. We would start a movie, only to wind up on my bed, the dialogue serving as background noise. This pattern continued through Thursday, our final night together.

The air was heavy, tensions high. Neither one of us was prepared to say goodbye.

We were lying in bed, curled up together. "Tomorrow," I sighed.

"Yeah." Micah's voice broke. "Would it be too much of me to ask for a parting gift?"

*A gift?* I stared blankly at him. "Sorry, was I supposed to get you something?"

He grinned. Fuck, how I was gonna miss that. "We never forget our firsts and I'd like to be yours." Micah choked up. "So, you know, you don't forget me."

"It's hard to forget your first love," I offered. What did I have to lose at this point? He was leaving no matter what we felt for each other.

In a blazing crush of lips, Micah claimed me. Whether we had sex or not, I was his, and I doubted my heart would ever find another. But that was my issue to work through, not his. It just wasn't our time, I guessed, or this wouldn't be ending.

When we came up for air, I swallowed down the nerves and asked, "How—how does this work exactly?"

Micah flashed that jaw-dropping smile of his. "Honestly? I want you inside me."

That surprised me. I thought for sure it would be the other way around, which had terrified me, though I'd have agreed to anything, no matter what Micah asked for.

"Show me what to do."

Micah hung over the side of the bed, snagging his jeans from the floor, and pulled a few packets from the pocket. My eyes nervously clocked his every move. "Condom and lube," he explained.

He placed the condom next to us, handed me a lube packet, then proceeded to open a second one and spread the gel over two fingers. After that, he reached behind himself. Curiosity got the best of me and I leaned forward, eager to see what he was doing.

"Holy shit," I whispered, and glanced up at Micah. Lips parted slightly, eyes heavily lidded and open just a slit. He was clearly enjoying this.

"See something you like?" He winked. I nodded far too eagerly. "Grab the other lube packet and the condom and slick up."

Eagerly, I opened the condom then stared down at it. I thought I knew what to do but my mind was...blank.

"Pinch the tip and roll it down your shaft," Micah directed. Thank fuck one of us had a functional brain right now. "Then slick it up."

That was the easy part. I was hard as a rock watching Micah prep himself. I could've easily come just like this, stroking myself while watching him finger his ass. I'd never seen anything hotter.

"Lie back, Jonah," Micah said. As soon as I was in position, he situated himself above me. "Hi." He leaned down and kissed me. "It's been a while since I've bottomed, so give me a sec to get used to the stretch."

I nodded, unsure what to say, let alone what to do. How would my dick fit in that tight space? How could that even feel good? My head was swimming with questions, much as it had been since I'd first laid eyes on Micah, but now wasn't the time. Sex now, Google later.

With one hand on my chest to brace himself, Micah reached around with the other, grabbed my cock, and slowly sank down on it.

Holy. Motherfucking. Hell.

It was like my dick was in a vise grip.

A sweet, *"please let me fuck you, please let me fuck you, you're so fucking hot"* vise grip.

Every drop of blood inside me rushed to my dick. This alone was likely going to force me to come on impact, which was the last thing I wanted. I needed to treasure this moment with Micah, store it away to draw from in times of need. Times when I truly missed him, which I knew would be inevitable. The angel and devil in my brain struggled for dominance, wreaking havoc in my mind. One demanded I stay still, do what Micah had requested, while the other screamed, *Thrust up! Thrust up!* I was terrified to move, scared I'd screw something up. Or worse, hurt Micah, and that was a hard *No* for me. He squeezed his eyes shut as he sat still on top of me, and I was afraid I had already broken him.

"Micah?" I whispered.

His eyes flew open, and he leaned over to claim my lips in a searing kiss. His tongue eagerly pushed its way inside. As it penetrated my mouth, his ass gripped my dick, taking me to heights I'd never imagined. Endorphins ran every which way, lighting pathways inside me that I'd never tread, and I couldn't control a single one of them.

"God, Micah," I said, as soon as I caught my breath. "You feel incredible."

"So do you."

I grabbed hold of his slender hips and thrust up as he bore down. I was inside of him as deep as I could go and never wanted to be free. This feeling, this culmination of two beings connected in such a magical way, was like nothing I'd ever felt before. The painful pressure inside me screamed for release. Against it, the need to hold it in as long as I could and savor every moment waged an internal battle. Neither side would win. Holding out would kill me but coming too soon would render this over, and that could be even worse.

If I thought Micah was gaining control of my heart before, this single act just sealed the deal. I was his. Even if we never saw each other again, Micah Hannigan would always have a place in my heart.

First kiss.

First sexual experience.

*First love.*

"Jonah," he panted, picking up the pace, "please tell me you're close."

"I was close the second I rolled the condom on."

"Need to, need to... come," Micah groaned out. I was caught between staring up at his beautiful face as he unraveled and watching as spurt after spurt burst forth and slid down his shaft. Some landed just below my navel. The image was framed like a piece of art and stored in my ever-growing memory.

I arched up, pushed as deeply as I could, and came. "Micah," ghosted across my lips as I filled the condom. Micah collapsed on top of me, and I wrapped my arms around him, needing him near as our bodies came down from the euphoric high. Eventually, I slid out, and we rolled to our sides, facing one another.

I kept my arms around him, as he did me. I never wanted to let go, never wanted to give Micah up. He was meant to be mine. Our bodies fit together like they were made for each other. We were completely spent, and wordlessly, we slowly began to drift off. Before my eyes shut all the way, I slipped out of bed, careful not to wake him, and wet a washcloth in the bathroom. I gently wiped away the remnants of our coupling, tossed the rag to the floor, and curled up around Micah. In no time, I was out.

Bright and early the next morning, Micah's phone went off. We dressed silently before I walked him back to his hotel. We hugged and kissed on the sidewalk until his phone rang again, then said our goodbyes. Solemnly, I made the short walk home, feeling as though I'd never breathe quite right again. Like I'd just handed over my heart, unable to function without it.

# Chpater Ten

**Micah**

I was miserable as fuck, tired as hell, and ready to hitch-hike back to Jonah at the next stop we made for gas.

This. Fucking. Sucked.

"Lunchtime!" Dad announced. Wasn't sure why he was so fucking chipper, but it grated on my last nerve.

"Seems like someone found puppy love," Mom teased. Dad reached over and took her hand, kissing her knuckles.

She stared lovingly back at him, and I hated it. Hated all happy people right now because my happy was taken away from me.

I groaned as they began singing some dumbass old song, belting out, "And they called it, puppy loooovvveeee."

Frustrated, I raked my hands over my face. "What is wrong with you people?"

"Quit sulking and text him already," Mom replied.

"Text?" I questioned like it was some unknown entity.

"Don't tell me Mister *I'm always glued to my phone* didn't have the forethought to exchange numbers with his summer love?" Dad said.

I groaned and mumbled, "Not summer love." Though I knew it was, it was also so much more than that, and I hated myself for leaving him. And I also knew, right at that very moment, that I was the world's biggest jackass for Not. Getting. Jonah's. Number!

"AHHHHH!" I screamed. "I'm so fucking stupid."

"Language, Micah," Mom warned before the three of them, whom I literally had just disowned in my mind, burst into uncontrollable fits of laughter.

"Glad to see the money we paid for your college tuition was well spent," Dad teased.

"Hardy, har, har. Real funny. I'm riding with a bunch of comedians." What sucked was how right he was. How could someone on the dean's list not remember to get a fucking phone number???

I stewed all the way to the hotel in Maryland, the same one we had stayed at on the drive up. Once inside the room, I tossed my suitcase on the bed, grabbed what I needed, and stormed into the bathroom, not giving Addy a chance to get there first. As the water heated up, I angrily stared at myself in the mirror. Even my reflection mocked me. *Dumbass.*

What the hell was I going to do?

The next day, we were midway through North Carolina when it hit me. I could call the restaurant. I kept trying to bring up Google on my phone, only for it to freeze up because we were driving through so many dead zones. The frustration mounted each time the damn spinning wheel of internet doom circled on my phone screen. It took all I had not to launch the damn thing out the window. But then I'd really be screwed.

By the time we got home, I was dead tired. I'd tried to call the restaurant no less than twenty-five times, and each attempt resulted in a busy signal. Either that was a bogus number online or the phone was off the hook. Considering the state my mind was in, reaching out again and maybe finally talking to an actual human being would've only resulted in an unpleasant conversation on both ends.

Not how I wanted it to go. I instead resigned myself to a shower and bed. *Alone.*

How could I miss him so much? Two days. One night. That was it, all we'd been apart, and I was already a wreck.

Saturday night, a little after ten p.m., and my lame ass was in my childhood bed. I tossed and turned, angrily punching my pillow as though it were the reason for my lack of sleep and foul mood. I finally fell asleep at about the same time the sun had risen, only to be woken up by the shrill sound of a ringtone I'd quickly be changing.

"What?" I growled in lieu of a cordial hello.

"Whoa, man. What crawled up your ass and died?" my friend Damon asked. We'd gone to high school together and now both attended FSU, where we'd been dormmates for the last three years.

"Sorry, just tired. What's up?" I half-assed apologized. I didn't really care what he thought but I was aware enough to know that it wasn't his fault I was angry at the world.

"Nada. Got back from the beach last night. Wanted to see if you had anything going on today that I could invite myself to," Damon said. I could hear him tossing a football around. Typical. Damon was on the school team, hoping to go pro. Rumor had it, that dream was likely to come true. Scouts had already been in contact with him.

"I have zero clue. Need to do laundry at some point. In desperate need of a quad shot," I admitted, already feeling the virtual caffeine hit my stream.

"Meet me at the Starbucks behind El Pollo Loco in twenty," Damon said and hung up.

I stared blankly at my phone. *WTF?*

I hopped in the shower and slid into the only clean pair of shorts I had, which were swim trunks. Oh, well. Found a clean shirt and flip-flops, grabbed my keys and wallet, and off I went.

Driving my Toyota Corolla, a high school graduation present from my parents, was almost as good as the cup of coffee I was about to inhale. *Almost.* Being in control of your own vehicle was such a sense of freedom. Having been trapped with the *Familia,* with Dad behind the wheel, for as long as I just had made me miss being my own man. Correction—made me miss being a solo driver in a solo vehicle.

"Dude," Damon said, drawing me into a one-armed bro-hug. "You missed some killer waves."

"Ugh, don't remind me." We gave the barista our orders and took a seat while they whipped up our drinks.

"Spill!" Damon more or less demanded.

"Michael, Damon?" the barista called out. I rolled my eyes when she mispronounced my name. Not the first time that's happened and likely not the last. We grabbed our drinks and sat back down.

"I sort of kinda met someone and I sort of kinda fucked up," I admitted, before taking the first sip. That warm, bean-infused bliss slid down the back of my throat. It was ...heaven.

"Um, how does that work exactly?" Damon questioned.

I told him the whole story, ending with my inability to have a fully functioning brain at the right time.

"Oh. My. God." His raucous, booming laughter drew attention as he nearly fell off his chair. I wish he had so I would be the one laughing instead. "Dude, that is the dumbest thing ever. How did you not get his number?"

"Saw each other almost every day. Spent most nights together. It was a ten-minute max walk to wherever he was. No need for phones. You do the math. To be honest, I only looked at my phone for the time of day, so I knew when to meet him at work, or to answer when my dad called. It was kind of nice not being married to technology for a week. Small-town America." I shrugged. It was true, the thought had never crossed my mind. Getting to wherever Jonah was, whether it be work or home, had been the key highlight of my days.

Damon finally got his asshole self under control. "Man, looking at how sad you are now, I almost feel bad for laughing. Almost. Have you tried to google-stalk him? Maybe that town has some online directory where you can find his address or some sort of home phone number?"

Wasn't a bad suggestion. I grabbed my phone and dialed the restaurant again. Fucking busy signal. When I slammed my phone down on the table, several heads turned our way. "I googled the number for his work, but every time I call it, I get a busy signal. It's like someone left it off the hook or something."

"Maybe," Damon replied, checking out a couple of females that came in. "There was so much ass in Daytona. Plenty of hot dudes too," he added for my benefit.

"There is only one ass I'm fixated on and it's all the way in Maine." I groaned. "When I get home, I'll see if I can find his home address or some other sort of lifeline to Jonah."

"Jonah, huh? Religious zealot?" he asked.

"Nah, not at all. Seriously totally cute-as-hell boy next door. Blond curls, blue eyes. Total dream," I said, picturing Jonah's dimples.

"Any pictures?"

"Shit." I leaned over, smacking my head against the tabletop. Damon, being the jackass that he was, just laughed.

"My friend, you are zero and two and, in my book, that is a major loss. Not a good rank. It's like you lost your A-game or something," Damon said, shaking his head in disbelief at me.

"I lost something alright." Just wasn't gonna let him know it was my heart.

We shot the shit and got caught up like we'd not seen each other in years even though it had only been a couple of weeks. When the coffee was gone, I told Damon I was gonna head home and get some shit done. He stayed behind and made his way over to the table of girls currently ogling him. I had to admit, he was hot as fuck with that overly worked-out running-back body of his. But he and I had only ever been and would only ever be friends. Damon was one hundred percent hetero male and I'd never been attracted to him. Now Jonah, on the other hand, was an instant attraction. I finally understood what insta-love was 'cause I got bitch-slapped sideways with it.

While my laundry was in its wash cycle, I booted up the laptop and searched every nook and cranny on the internet for Jonah. It was like the entire town of Stoney Brook didn't exist. Sure, you could find restaurants, hotels, info about the festival. Nothing about the residents though. It was so odd and furthered my frustration—like, to epic proportions. A massive blowup was on the horizon for me.

I even called the Stoney Brook Inn, only to be told they couldn't give out that kind of information.

*Would I ever get to see Jonah again?*

A couple of weeks passed by and suddenly it was time to load up my car and head back to the dorms. I'd finally resigned myself to giving up after making one last attempt.

"Ahoy Matey's, this is Stuart. How may I help you?"

Silently, I fist-bumped the air. "Yes, Stuart. Hello. I need to speak to Jonah, please."

"Jonah doesn't work here anymore. Can I help you?"

My heart dropped. Like literally fell out of my chest and rolled under my shoes for me to stomp on.

"No thanks," I muttered and hung up.

# CHAPTER ELEVEN

**Jonah**

"Jonah, can you come here a second, please?" Dad hollered up the stairs.

It had been a month since Micah left, and I'd hardly said a word to anyone, just went through the daily grind in an emotionless, robotic mode.

"Have a seat." Dad gestured to my usual spot at the kitchen table, next to where Mom already sat. She reached over and squeezed my hand. "We need to talk, son." Dad pulled out his chair and joined us. "Jonah, your mother and I have made our decision. We've decided it's best to sell the business and the house, move to Florida before winter hits."

"Wait, what?" I asked, feeling a bit blindsided. They hadn't mentioned Florida since that very first time before the Tall Ships Festival. "What does that mean for me?" Were they leaving me behind? "Where would I go? Who could I live with?" Jim would probably hire me but that still would leave Sadie and me homeless.

"Jonah." Mom patted my hand again. "Stop panicking, you're coming with us."

"Oh, thank fuck." I breathed a sigh of relief, then realized what I'd said. "Oh, crap. I'm so sorry."

"Jonah, you're nearly twenty. It's not like we're gonna ground you for using foul language. But I would like to ask you refrain as much as you can," Dad replied.

"Yes, sir."

"Now, where was I?"

"Florida, dear," Mom reminded him.

"Ah yes, Florida. One of the families that were in town visiting for the Tall Ships Festival decided this is where they'd like to raise their young ones. Something about Silicon Valley being too fast-paced and plastic. Not sure what that meant, but they bought the restaurant and the house. Your mother and I are flying to Florida this weekend to look at a couple of homes that a real estate agent we've been in contact with set up for us to tour. Stuart will be running the shop. The new owners have asked him to stay on as their manager, so unless there's an emergency and he needs your expertise, you have the weekend off."

Sadie and I had never been left alone in the house for that long. I wished Micah was still in town, it would have been great to spend the weekend with him. Naked flesh wound together beneath the sheets, being inside him again. I understood now how some people could become addicted to sex. It was beyond words. Or maybe it was just the man I had shared those experiences with. I should've asked for his number, but I figured he would have given it to me if he wanted me to have it. I needed to man up and accept that I was only a summer fling, a meaningless way to pass the time. For him, at least. For me? Well, my heart never received that message.

"We'll leave you some money so you and Sadie can get pizza or whatever. The fridge is full too," Mom said. I, as usual, remained silent.

"Might want to spend the time packing up your room. It'll be about a month before we leave, and that's only if we find a house we like. At least we'll be paying cash, so hopefully, we can get a quick close," Dad said, setting his cup in the sink. "Mom and I fly out tomorrow and will be back late Sunday."

I managed a nod but didn't have much more in me past that. Sadie and I went out back to enjoy the afternoon sun and give me some time to think. Before long, it would be cold, but thankfully we wouldn't be here for that. As it had been since Micah left, my every waking thought was filled with him. His smile, those gorgeous eyes staring back at me. How mad he got when he lost a video game yet still managed to look cute as hell. Even in his semi-joking fury, he brought color to my life. He was so full of life and woke up my sleepy world, made it bright. He was like a little kid wanting to check out all the new sights and sounds. Sadie adored him, just like me.

Maybe when I got to Florida, I could buy my own car. There's freedom in that. Get out on the open road, enjoy the sites, meet new people. Of course, I'd most likely need one to get a job anyway. I was sure nothing would be as walkable as it was in Stoney Brook.

Was it weird to be excitedly nervous? Was that even a thing? I was excited to have survived my last frozen winter, but nervous about starting my life over. What if Micah came looking for me, only to find I was gone?

*Wishful thinking, Jonah. You're nothing more than a blip on his radar. Another face in the sea of hookups.*

So many new experiences were ahead of me. I'd never been outside of Maine, so I was looking forward to the drive down to Florida, seeing the sights along the way. And I seriously couldn't wait to wear shorts year-round.

I walked over to my old swing set and noticed that the wood needed resealing. It'd been unused for so long that I felt guilty. I was sure the kids moving in would breathe new life into the old toy that had brought me so much joy and now sat idly. I decided that, while Mom and Dad were gone to look at houses, I'd grab the sander and sealant from the garage and spruce it up for the new family that would be moving in here.

"Jonah, dinner," Mom called out.

"Coming, Mom."

My parents left bright and early the next morning. Sadie and I said our goodbyes, then went back to bed. They called when they landed and reported that they were already enjoying the warmth but weren't too fond of the humidity. I had to laugh, telling them there was a tradeoff for every season. Snow looks great but sucks to shovel. Warmth is great but the humidity in the South sucks. Nothing is perfect, you just have to pick and choose your battles or in this case, climate.

After we hung up, Sadie and I took a walk along the waterfront and passed Ahoy Matey's. I stood there for a few minutes, staring up at the building I was so familiar with. Where I'd spent my life, basically. I knew I would miss it, but I had no regrets about being practically raised inside the red and white walls. I had learned so much working there alongside my folks, but I agreed with them, it was time to move on. Without a doubt, I knew Florida had bigger, better things in store for me.

Mom and Dad called a couple of times over the weekend and texted pics of the houses they'd seen. I laughed whenever they did, realizing the agent must've shown them how to use that feature because they'd never done that before. In between calls, I worked on the swing set. On Sunday afternoon, they called just as I was cleaning up—I was proud with the way the swing set turned out but damn tired—and walked me through the pictures and layouts they had sent, and together we selected a home. Our next home. They made an offer on the house and then boarded the plane back to Maine.

"Now we wait," Mom said to me when they got home. "They have twenty-four hours to respond, and the agent said it was a pretty hot market out there, so we opted for a full-price offer."

"We have backups, though," Dad chimed in. "If they're still available, that is."

"We'll figure it out, Dad. So, what's the plan of attack? Are we bringing everything with us or..." I trailed off, leaving it up to them to finish.

Mom said, "Only the family heirlooms come with, and personal items. Couches in the living room and family room are getting donated. The bedroom sets, dining table, and hutch are going with. Most have been in the family for generations. The couch in your room is the oldest one, so I'd suggest donating it as well."

"Yeah, I agree. If we get this house, will my wall unit fit in my new bedroom?" I asked.

"Oh, I'm not so sure," Mom replied. "I'll leave that up to you. If you want it to come, it comes. No reason for you to have to get rid of your things when we're the ones deciding it's time to move on."

"Hey, come outside, I want to show you something." I stood, gesturing for my parents to follow.

"Oh, Jonah," Mom sighed when she saw the refurbished swing set. "This is just lovely."

"Son," Dad patted my shoulder, "words escape me. Such a thoughtful gesture for the new family."

"I was thinking, I have enough in my savings to buy a car. I hope I do, at least. Could we maybe look for one once we get settled in?" I asked them. Mom nodded to Dad, their usual silent speaking going on.

"We thought we'd buy you a car when we got down there. You're giving up everything and taking a chance with the old folks." Dad smiled. "Thought it would be a nice treat for you."

On the inside, I was dancing like a monkey, but I didn't want to freak them out by doing it for real. Instead, I grinned widely. "Thanks. I'm super excited about the move."

Just then, Dad's phone rang. "Hello?" He turned to Mom. "It's the agent."

"Put her on speakerphone," Mom told him, and he stared blankly back at her. I reached over and hit the speaker button for him.

"Joan, Michael, Jonah, welcome to Florida! You just bought yourself a house!" she announced. Mom clapped, I ran over and hugged her, and Dad whooped. "I guess that means you're happy?" the agent added. I could tell she was smiling just from the tone in her voice. "I'll get the documents ready for you to sign and will send them via email. The home inspection will happen in the next week. I'll call you tomorrow after I send the docs to make sure you received them. Congratulations!"

The next few weeks were a whirlwind of both packing what we were taking and hauling away things we didn't need to the local thrift store. It was the only donation center in town, but Sarah, the woman who ran it, was happy to accept our items. Poor Sadie-girl was confused as stuff kept leaving the house. I did my best to reassure her that everything was alright, but she was glued to my side like she thought I'd leave her too.

When the movers came and loaded up their truck was when reality hit. This was goodbye to all I'd ever known. All my parents had known, too, both having been born and raised here as well. We filled our van to the brim with what we needed and as we drove through town on our way out, everyone we knew stood alongside the road to wave goodbye. It was a bittersweet send-off, the three of us teary-eyed, waving back as we bid a final farewell to the town we knew and loved. The town and its residents that had supported us as we had them.

The places I took Micah to. The streetlights outside his hotel where we first kissed. The cove hidden deeply behind my house where we shared more than that. My bedroom where I lost my virginity. I regretted nothing and left the place with only fond memories, although the realization that I'd never share another with Micah made me depressed. Maybe it was best to move away, maybe the heartbreak would dissipate.

We took our time driving down the coast since the movers said it would take them a week to get our stuff to us anyway. We stopped in every state, seeing as much as we could, and Mom collected a state-shaped magnet from each one for her new refrigerator. I vowed to myself that one day I'd see all fifty states. Visit each national monument, cruise down the Pacific Coast Highway, stop along the way to touch the ocean so I could say I'd been to both. My mind was an endless maze of bucket-list items and places to visit. The world was at my fingertips, I just needed to reach out and grasp it.

I knew it was time for me to shake off the melancholy, to stop being sad.

This was a time of rebirth, a time to reinvent myself.

To find out what made Jonah tick.

A time for Jonah Thomas to find his place in this world.

We arrived at our new house the night before the movers did and without our beds, so we had to stay at a hotel. Bright and early the next morning, we went to see our new home.

"Wow!" I said, taking in the wall-to-wall ceramic tile. Having grown up with the warmth of carpet, this was quite the paradigm shift. It was a single-story home, an anomaly in Stoney Brook, where all the houses had two floors. My parents' bedroom was on one end, my room and a guest room on the other and separated by a shared bathroom. The kitchen, dining, and living rooms were between my parents' room and mine. A split-floor plan, my dad explained to me. A wall of sliding glass doors led out to an enclosed pool area, or *lanai,* as the real estate agent had told my parents it was called. The top and sides were screened in, which provided uninhibited views of the water and lush landscaping. This water dog was in love with it already.

"I can't believe we have a pool. This is beyond awesome!" I called out, leaning over to run my hand through the water. "It's the perfect temperature."

Directly behind the outdoor space was a lake with a water fountain in the center. I could see a sign from here that read, "Beware of alligators."

"Dad?" I asked, pointing to it.

"Yes, son. Alligators are a real thing here. You'll need to keep Sadie on a leash and away from the water unless you're at the ocean. All other areas are likely to have gators," Dad replied.

"Holy crap."

"Holy crap is right." Dad laughed. "What do you think of the house?"

There was so much to take in. From the lush, green landscaping, so different from the greenery in Maine, to the stucco exterior, to the tile. This house was one hundred percent *not* what you would find in Maine. It was like a whole new world for me, like we had changed countries instead of states. It blew my mind how things could be so different yet still be part of the United States. "I like it, a lot."

By the time we unloaded the van, the movers had arrived. Mom headed to the grocery store that we'd passed on the way in while Dad and I stayed behind. The rest of the day was spent directing them where to place things, then we set up our beds and crashed hard. Even Ms. Sadie didn't stir all night, having sniffed her heart out all day long. So many new scents for her to get familiar with, and chasing geckos seemed to be her new thing.

It took us about a week to get settled in and unpack the massive number of boxes, and a couple of days after that, we went car shopping. I was like a kid in a candy store, with so many to choose from. Thankfully, Dad was the voice of reason because I was ready to buy the first one we looked at. We settled on a used Toyota Camry that had only one prior owner and very low mileage. It was great. I talked Dad into letting me take it out and drive around town, promising to use the navigation system the car came with.

I told them I'd pick up dinner, on me, and when I asked what they'd like to eat, they told me to surprise them.

I found a strip mall with a couple of restaurants in it and decided I wanted Asian cuisine for dinner. As I drove past a stand-alone chain restaurant in the parking lot, I spotted a "Now Hiring" sign in the window. I didn't have a resume with me—hadn't thought to make one, to be honest—but felt I couldn't pass up this opportunity. Especially now that I had gas and car insurance to pay for.

"Hello, welcome to Sam's Town. Would you like to sit in the bar area or a booth?" the hostess asked.

"Oh um, no thank you. I'm here about the sign in the window. Could I fill out an application?" I nearly stuttered with how nervous I was.

"Let me get the manager for you," she said, disappearing around the corner.

I stood in the lobby and shifted from foot to foot, realizing I was nowhere near dressed appropriately for an interview. Shortly after she left, an older gentleman appeared from the same direction. "Are you here about the busboy job?" he asked.

"Yes, sir." I wasn't sure what the job was for, but any job was better than no job. "I'm Jonah," I said, extending my hand.

"I'm Sam, owner of this particular Sam's Town. Name thing was not intentional. You got a minute to sit and chat?"

"Yes, sir."

We walked through the lobby, past the bar, and through the kitchen to a small office area similar to the one my parents had at Ahoy Matey's. "Have a seat, Jonah." He gestured to the only other chair in the small space, having already taken the one behind the desk. "Tell me about your restaurant experience."

I dazzled him with the account of my burger-slinging career. And by dazzled, I mean he sat quietly, just taking it all in, as I most likely bored him to death with far too many details.

"Well, Jonah, I don't normally do this, but I have a good feeling about you. Job pays minimum wage and it's part-time. Do you have any problem with shift work, or days and times you're not available?" Sam asked.

"No, sir. I can work any time, day or night."

"Alright. How about you come back Monday at ten a.m.? We'll get you started on paperwork before training." Sam stood. "Welcome to the Sam's Town team."

Elated, I shook his hand and thanked him. When I got inside the car I screamed in delight, banging the steering wheel, and accidentally set off the horn. When I looked up,

Sam and the hostess were staring through the window at me. Sam was shaking his head but smiled. I waved at them and drove off before I could embarrass myself any further, and decided to pick up dinner from a different area.

"Jonah, you were gone quite a while. I was afraid you got lost," Mom said as I stepped inside.

"Nope." I smiled wide. "I got a job!"

"Jonah!" Mom cheered, hugging me.

Dad came up beside us and patted my shoulder. "Congratulations. Let's sit down to dinner and you can tell us all about it. I'm starving."

It was a Friday night, and Sam's Town was packed. I'd worked there for a few weeks now, and Sam was pleased with my performance, saying he'd be moving me into a server position by the end of the month. A rowdy group of guys had sat down in the bar area, but I had my back to them as I helped our bartender, Monica, restock the freshly washed glasses.

"Jonah?" someone said. The voice sounded familiar, so I figured it was one of the regulars, but when I turned around, Micah was standing there. The stunned look on his face surely matched mine.

I was numb, standing still as a statue at the sight of him, until Monica nudged me. "Go say hi. He's got a smile a mile wide for you, sweetie." It'd taken me a while to get used to what I was told was southern charm. The *sweeties*, *honeys*, and *darlings* coming out in various twangs had thrown me at first, though I'd quickly grown to love it. I wiped my hands on the towel I was using and stepped around the bar. Micah immediately swept me off my feet and swung me around. Not sure how he managed that since we were both the same height and I was even slightly wider than him.

"Jonah, my God, I missed you so fucking much. I've looked all over for you. I called the restaurant a million times, then some guy told me you didn't work there anymore. I thought I lost you forever." He cupped my face in his hands and leaned in and kissed me. His friends whooped and hollered from a nearby table. My face was on fire and I smiled so wide I thought my cheeks would split. I was so fucking happy I wanted to scream!

"Get his number!" one of his friends called out.

"Oh, yeah! Jonah, give me your phone," Micah said.

"Why?" I knew why, but I was so fucking nervous I blurted the stupid question out without thinking first.

"I don't want to lose track of my boyfriend again."

"Boyfriend?" I questioned, handing him my new phone.

He tapped away and I immediately heard his chime in his pocket. "Yes, boyfriend." He took me by the hand and practically dragged me over to his table. "Everyone, this is Jonah. My Jonah. I mean…" Seemed even he was a bit nervous now. Micah turned to me, his smile as big as the moon. "My boyfriend, Jonah."

"How did you know where to find me?" I asked.

"Find you? I didn't know you were even here. Like I said, I searched every inch of the internet, stalking you, and came up blank. I came home for the weekend and my friends and I usually hang out here when we're all in town. I can't fucking believe I finally found you," Micah said as he drew me in for another kiss. His friends howled at us in the background.

"Is it okay to say I missed you?" I timidly asked.

"Babe," he took my face in his hands, "I missed you more than words can explain."

Six months later…

"Jonah, come on, put your back into it," Micah complained.

"Ugh, I'm trying. This damn thing is too heavy, and it's hotter than Hades' taint," I replied, surely working on a hernia or two.

Micah laughed, damn near dropping it. "Come on, we're almost there." Micah tugged his end and groaned.

"Why. Is. It. So. Big." I paused, wiping the sweat from my brow.

"Because it is. Now come on. Push!"

"Ahhhh!" we both cried out. He pushed and I pulled at the same time, and we damn near launched it into the living room, having used far more force than was needed. As soon as it was in place, we collapsed on top of the sofa Micah's parents had given us.

"Our first place," Micah said, holding his hand out.

I placed mine in his. "Our first place."

It wasn't much, just a small one-bedroom up three long-ass flights of stairs. June in Orlando was not a fun time to move. I'd underestimated my ability to handle the combination of heat and humidity. Not something I'd likely do again.

Micah had landed a job with an accounting firm straight out of college, one that he started on Monday, and the office was just outside of Orlando. Both our families were helping us move in this weekend, which was great. Addy had decided to stay with one of her friends for the night, and Micah said she'd only be in the way if she was here anyway, but I could tell he missed her. The moms had spent some time shopping together beforehand, deciding they would take care of what we needed. Neither of us really cared about anything outside of being together, so we let them bond over decorating our ten-foot by ten-foot apartment.

Okay, It was actually bigger than that, but not by much.

I was on the hunt for a new job. I hated leaving Sam's Town, but the drive was too far, and Sam understood that. Said he'd give a great reference to anyone who called him. I really liked working for him. He gave a small-town boy his first chance out in the real world, and I'd never forget that. Everyone on the staff was great to work alongside, too, and I'd miss them all.

This was my first time not living with my parents, and I was back to that excitedly nervous thing again. Nervous over leaving the parental clutch, excited to start a new life with the man who owned my heart. My parents were only a ninety-minute drive away, so it wasn't like I couldn't see them or vice versa. Either way, we were a family and we'd make it work.

Micah's mother said she'd never seen him happier and claimed it was because of me. I wasn't so sure about that, but I was doing my best to take it all in stride. My life had undergone a ton of changes since Micah and I met and I knew there was still a lot more in store for me. With Micah by my side, anything was possible.

Later that night, after our parents went home, we started unpacking. We were thankful for all their help, the dads having put the bed together along with a bookshelf. No one batted an eye or commented about us sharing a bed.

The parents seemed just as happy as Micah and I were, which is the way it should be. The moms had unpacked and cleaned the kitchen supplies they bought us, as well as washed the new sheets and made up the bed. Without their help, we would have spent our first night in our new place on the floor. What can I say? We could pretty much crash anywhere but the moms weren't having any of that.

"I can't wait for Mom and Dad to bring Sadie to us tomorrow," I said, opening another box.

"Same. I miss that sweet girl. Is that...?" Micah said, pointing to my hand.

The fond memories associated with what I clutched would forever be a happy place for me that I'd draw from every time I saw it. It was a part of me and Micah and I'd never let it go. "It is."

"The blanket from the cove," Micah said, running his hand over it.

I laid it out across the back of the couch. "Our blanket. It belongs with us."

Who knew a summer romance would turn into this summer boy's dream forever?

# ABOUT THE AUTHOR

TL Travis is an award-winning published author of LGBTQIA+ contemporary and paranormal romance and erotic musings that have earned "Best-Selling Author" flags in the US as well as Internationally.

In her free time, TL enjoys catching up with her family, attending concerts, wine tasting, and traveling.

# Also By

**The Social Sinners Series:**

<u>**Boxset:**</u>

https://books2read.com/SSWorldTour

**Behind the Lights, 1**

MM Coming of Age Rockstar Romance

**In the Shadows, 2**

MM Rockstar Hurt/Comfort Romance

**A Heart Divided, 3**

MMM Rockstar Romance

**Beyond the Curtain, 4**

MM BDSM Hurt/Comfort PTSD Rockstar Romance

**After the Final Curtain, 5**

MM BDSM Rockstar Romance

**Maiden Voyage Series:**

**Boxset**

**Ryder's Guardian, 1**

MM Rockstar Bodyguard Romance

**Derek's Destiny, 2**

MM Rockstar Teacher Romance

**Jaxson's Nemesis, 3**

MM Enemies to lovers Rockstar Romance

**Shadow's Light, 4**

MM Rockstar Hurt/Comfort Second Chance Romance

**Embrace The Fear (ETF) Series:**

**Rhone's Rebel, 1**

MM Hurt/Comfort Rockstar Romance

**David's Disaster, 2**

MM Daddy-boy Hurt/Comfort Rockstar Romance

**Seltzer's Taylor, 3**

11/3/2023

MM Rockstar Romance

**His Final Chase, 4**

MM Rockstar Daddy-Little Romance

11/2024

**Daddies and their Littles**

When Daddy Hurts

MM Daddy-Little Hurt/Comfort Romance

## A Little Christmas: Jacob

MM Daddy-Little Hurt/Comfort Romance

A Little Christmas: Orion's Secret

MM Daddy-Little Hurt/Comfort Romance

## <u>Pet Play</u>

Pick Us, Daddy

Pride Pet Play 2023 Series

https://books2read.com/PPP2023

## <u>Standalone novels:</u>

### Heat

MM Small Town Coming of Age Bear Bottom Romance

### Only Time Will Tell

MM Coming of Age Time-Travel Romance

### See Me

MM Hurt/Comfort Enemies to Lovers Body Positive/Disfigurement Romance

## <u>Greyson Fox Saga (each can be read as a standalone):</u>

### Greyson Fox

MM Erotic May/December Age-Gap First Time Coming of Age Romance

### Forgive Me Father

MM Coming of Age Hurt/Comfort Rent-a-boy Romance

## Stand-alone novelette's/novella's:

### Summer Boy

MM Small Town First-Time Coming of Age Demisexual Romance

### Girl Crush

MF (1 scene)/ FF Sapphic Romance

### What Works For Us

FF Over 40 Erotic Novelette

### Rules of the Game

MM Erotic Workplace Romance

### Coffee, Tea or Me?

MM Contemporary Romance

### Penny For Your Thoughts

MM Contemporary Second Chance Holiday Romance

## Paranormal Romance:

### The Sebastian Chronicles

Historical Paranormal Erotic Romance

(Includes all 5 stories listed below)

### Sebastian, The Beginning

MF Historical Paranormal Erotica

### My Servant, My Lover

MF/MM Historical Paranormal Erotica

### Wealthy Ménage

MF/MM/MFM/Ménage Historical Paranormal Erotica

**Prohibition Inhibitions**

MF/MM/MMF/MFM/BDSM Historical Paranormal

Erotica

**The Tryst - Chronicle Finale**

MM Paranormal Erotic Romance

**Pity the Living, Not the Dead**

MM Paranormal First Time Dark Romance

**MF Titles are published under Raven Kitts**

Milton Keynes UK
Ingram Content Group UK Ltd.
UKHW010744180923
428890UK00001B/22